Kate Alanna

Kate and Tansy Malone, fleeing from the 1847 Irish potato famine, find a refuge of a kind in a Liverpool tavern run by Malachy O'Leary. But Kate is delicate, and Tansy, ever anxious to protect her sister, sets out to try and better their situation.

In her struggle, Tansy meets many who help and hinder h·· Donal, the fiddler, whose dreams turn to dust. J········ ·merican, in search of a bride. And C············· ······ ···eper, who grieve···

Ta············ ···· ···· ··· ·er wits again··· ··· ·· ··· ···· ·· ·····g with Irish ··· ·· ·· ··· ··· ···· ··ctre of chol··

In the ··· ··· ··· ···· ·ulties lies both heartache and ···· ··· ··· ·· greatest adventure.

(The novel, complete within itself, is the second part of a trilogy about the Malones.)

Maureen Peters

Kate Alanna

m x.

ROBERT HALE & COMPANY
63 Old Brompton Road, London, S.W.7.

©   *Maureen Peters 1975*
First published in Great Britain 1975

ISBN 0 7091 46647

02792993

17631941

Printed in Great Britain by
Clarke, Doble & Brendon Ltd.,
Plymouth.

ONE

It was cold in the bowels of the ship; even though they were packed so closely together there was scarcely room to move. Tansy had long since grown used to the rocking motion and to the creaking of the timbers as the vessel ploughed her way across the Irish sea. It was more difficult to accustom oneself to the foetid, urine-soaked air and to the gloom that was relieved only by an occasional finger of light from the gaps in the planks above her head. In this heavy twilight, whispers, prayers, and the fretful wailing of children rose up unavailingly; but after twelve hours at sea the whispers had dwindled, the prayers had fallen back unheard, the sobbing of the little ones was muted.

She shifted her arm cautiously so as not to disturb the sleeping Kate who huddled in exhaustion next to her, and glanced longingly towards the wooden water tub. She had drunk copiously already but now her throat was parched again, her lips cracked. If she could step over Kate and make her way between the rows of dimly outlined figures — but when she made the effort her head spun and she leaned back, retching a little.

5

It seemed an eternity since they had boarded the ship at Dublin. Perhaps it *was* an eternity and they were all dead already; or perhaps it was merely a dream and she would wake presently to the sound of Granda calling her from the field. But Granda was dead along with the others. Only she and Kate were left, tied together by love and by necessity.

"This is the month of August in the year eighteen hundred and forty-seven," she mouthed silently. She had no idea what day it was, nor when they would reach Liverpool. Perhaps none of them would ever see land again, but would continue to sail on through the darkness for ever. A little shudder ran through her frame.

"Are you cold? Take my coat."

The voice at her other side was friendly and concerned. A warm weight descended on her shoulders.

"You're very kind."

She turned her head, narrowing her eyes against the dizziness, and saw a boy's thin face, greenish-white under a thatch of brown hair. Across the boy's knees lay a battered, oddly-shaped case.

"That's my fiddle." He had noticed her flickering glance. "I'm Donal, the fiddler."

"Tansy Malone O'Faolain." She indicated the sleeping Kate. "That's my sister."

"From?"

"Perimara. You'll not have heard of the village. It's about forty miles west of Dublin. And you?"

"From Connemara," he said, and it was sufficient.

It was well-known that the potato famine had hit hardest in the extreme west.

"Are you alone?"

"Orphaned these fifteen years." He gave her a crooked grin.

She saw now that he was older than she had at first supposed. The hunger that wizened babies had sharpened his features into an illusion of youth. The hands resting on the fiddle case were a man's hands grown past the protruding wristbones and skinned knuckles of a lad.

"Will you play the fiddle in Liverpool?" she asked.

"I'll play it in hell if the devil gives me a fee," he told her, and hearing her convulsive swallow as she fought against the pain of laughter, he said in quick, heartwarming concern, "Shall I be getting you a mug of water?"

She nodded, and he shifted the case over to her lap, and crawled crabwise to the water-butt.

"Here. Drink it."

The tin mug rattled against her teeth, but the water was cool and fresh.

Against her conscious will she began to speak.

"We had a cabin and land at Perimara. It was rented from Sir John Devereux, and we grew potatoes and barley, and Bridie had a vegetable garden. Bridie was my sister, but she's dead now. My Granda lived with us, and my brothers, Pat and Seamus. We never left our rent hanging. And then the famine came. All our crops turned black in a night. Seamus took the rent money and went to Dublin with his wife. We'll never see the pair of them again."

"Wouldn't your landlord help?"

"Sir John died," she said dully, "and Mr. Raleigh was too interested in marrying a rich wife to have time for our troubles."

7

"Mr. Raleigh?"

"His son. He was young and sweet-spoken, but he wouldn't help us. We left our rent hanging then for the first time, and the men came from Dublin with guns and burned the cabin and trampled the garden. Granda died in the fire, and Bridie died soon afterwards. She was the oldest and the strongest, but she lay down and turned her face to the wall, and died."

"Couldn't your other brother help?"

"Pat? He broke into the big house — into Devereux Place — but the men from Dublin shot him. Then there was just Kate and me."

"What of your husband?"

"Husband?" For a moment she looked at him without understanding.

"You wear a wedding ring."

"Oh, yes; Michael."

She glanced down at the dull circle that hung loosely upon her finger. Its yellow was already tarnished.

"Michael was hanged a few days ago," she said, almost indifferently. "He stole some silver from Devereux Place and tried to sell it in Dublin. They hanged him just before Kate and I got there."

"You're too young to be a widow," Donal said.

"I'm sixteen."

There was a kind of surprise in her voice. In her marriage to Michael O'Faolain she had never really felt like a wife. It was inconceivable to her that she was now a widow.

"Michael was a neighbour of ours," she said hesitantly. "He was a kindly man, not given to drinking or fighting. I was fond of him, and a girl has to marry somebody."

8

If she cannot have the man she wants, her thoughts ran on. But not for worlds could she have confided in this stranger about her childish admiration for the landowner's son. Raleigh Devereux had been the first English gentleman she had ever seen, and his elegance had dazzled her. But when the famine began she had seen the cold heart beneath the friendly smile and her infatuation had withered as swiftly as the potato crops.

"So now there is Kate," Donal said, his quiet voice prodding her into the present again.

"She's not strong. She never has been strong, though she's two years older than I am," Tansy said, very low.

"So you're off to Liverpool to seek your fortune, the two of you! Have you any notions about what you'll be doing there?"

"I can read and write," she said proudly. "Father MacNabb showed me how to do it. I used to go up to the presbytery every morning and learn there."

"Isn't that a marvellous thing now!" he said in admiration. "And why would a pretty girl like you want to learn the reading and writing?"

"To get on in the world." Her voice warmed into an almost forgotten enthusiasm. "Ever since I was a little girl I've wanted to travel, to see lands beyond Perimara. Granda said it was because, long ago, a girl came from the Viking country to marry a Malone. That's why Kate and I have yellow hair. But Kate was always content at home. In me there was a yearning, like a hunger, wanting to carry my feet past the potato fields. So I learned to read and write as a first step; but the famine came and scattered us all anyway. Have you ever been out of Ireland before?"

He shook his head.

"Connemara was my world, but it'll be a grand adventure to see another place. Have you lodgings to go to?"

It was Tansy's turn to shake her head.

"No more have I!" Donal said cheerfully. "But there'll be beds in plenty as it's such a big port. Work too."

"Especially for you and your fiddle," Tansy agreed.

"And you with your reading and writing. What does your sister do?"

"Do?" Tansy frowned slightly. "Why, she can mend neatly. Kate's always done the mending. Bridie used to cook and clean, and I helped Granda in the fields. Kate was always the beautiful one. Kate *is!*"

"Being and doing," he mused. "I wonder which is better. Will you be seeking work at a school then?"

"A school? Faith, I'm not clever enough yet!" she exclaimed, and felt a promise within herself as if she had taken some private vow to continue studying.

"Have you any money?" Donal whispered in her ear. "You'll be needing a few coppers for a bite and a bed. I can let you have a shilling."

"I don't need it," she whispered back hastily. "I have some shillings."

She had always been a good liar and it was too dim for him to see her expression. After a while she leaned her head against the wooden bulwark and let herself drift into an uneasy sleep.

Time passed in a series of flashes of wakefulness and periods of dark. In the dark she saw scenes of her life unfold and move before her as if she watched them from a high gallery in some deserted theatre of her mind. When she woke, the gloom and the rocking motion made her suspect she was still dreaming.

"Is it much longer to go?" Kate moaned softly, pulling herself into a sitting position.

"I don't think so. It'll be night again when we arrive probably."

"We'll never find our way in the big city," Kate whispered.

"Surely we will! Won't all the streets and the squares be marked with their names as it was in Dublin; and won't I be reading them out to you as we go along?"

"Can you keep your voice lower?" another voice hissed. "There's a woman here dying, and God help her but she has the right to do it in peace and quiet!"

"Surely the poor soul will be getting enough of that where she's going?" another voice argued.

"Not if she cannot make confession," another said. "Hasn't she been asking for a priest for hours?"

"And not one on this boat to lift her sins from her soul, and the poor woman twice widowed and owing a guinea to her daughter-in-law!"

Tansy could discern the group now, huddled around a shape that lay as still as if it were already a corpse, save for the thinly rasping breaths that fought their way into the stifling air.

At the other side the fiddler stirred, set down his case, and edged his way towards them.

"I can hear your confession." His voice came out strong and confident above the murmurings.

Tansy could see him, bending over the figure, his ear to

its mouth. The group had drawn back, pressed together to allow him space.

"Mercy on us, but he's pretending to be a priest," Kate whispered. "Isn't that the most shocking thing!"

"The most beautiful thing!" Tansy whispered back.

There was a stinging behind her eyes and a peace at her heart.

The rasping breaths had ceased and for an instant only the creaking of the timbers troubled the silence.

"She died at peace," a woman said. "Surely it was a sweet lie that sent her down the dark river."

"And surely she'll not be required to pay back the guinea now."

"Are you truly not of the cloth? Now isn't that a crying pity! We might have had a wedding to follow the wake."

The moment had passed, and a bitter humour salted the sweet mourning.

Donal crawled back to his place and leaned his head against the wood. In that instant there clung about him some of the mystery of death, as if, in passing, it had brushed him with his wings. Then he snapped open the fiddle case, and within a moment a thin and wavering melody stole into the air, each long drawn-out note seeming to hand like a question mark over the renewed whispering.

"I had a husband in Donegal, but he came over to find work. I'm hoping he's not found another woman as well."

"My own man died of the fever six weeks ago. I've a married sister in Ormskirk, who'll give me a place."

"My little girl was coming with me, but she had not the

will to walk the long miles. I tried to carry her, but she grew heavy as a stone. God forgive me, but there are only two sticks to mark where she lies."

"I sent my own boys north when this began, but the English set them to digging holes in the road, and then filling them up again."

"Now isn't that a typically English way to behave! Surely God never created a race with so little sense!"

Tansy slept again, treading in her dreams the green paths of Perimara, seeing the smoke curl up lazily from the whitewashed cabin, hearing the mingled voices of her family.

"Tansy Malone, will you take your filthy feet out of my clean kitchen!"

That had been Bridie, forever scrubbing and cleaning and cooking, and at the last, lying with closed eyes and hands that twitched as if they sought brush and pail and frying pan.

"Tansy, I've built another room to my cabin; and the pig has her own sty, so we can be wed when you choose."

Michael, with his long face and his shy smile that had irritated her so much when he was alive and now was grown so dim and meaningless.

"Tansy, of all my grandchildren, you are the one most like my Kathleen."

That was Granda, tall and gnarled with a pipe in his mouth that seemed like part of himself and a stubborn, tender look in his eyes.

"Tansy, the boat has stopped. We're here, I think!"

Kate was shaking her into full consciousness, and the voices died away.

13

Tansy dug her fists into her eyes and winced as she moved her cramped limbs. Overhead were running footsteps and shouted commands. Within the hold people were stretching and yawning, gathering together bags and bundles, stooping under the dark beams. A baby began to cry fretfully, its wails mingling with the buzz of conversation.

"Glory be to God, but my feet ache for dry land!"

"My brother promised me he'd meet me, but I'm not certain he'll know where to come."

"Someone must tell the captain about the poor soul down here. She'll be stinking out the hold in a couple of hours."

"We'll be going our ways in a moment. Shall I be seeing you again?"

Donal was at her side, his fiddle case clutched close.

"Surely there's a good chance of it, God willing! You must take your coat, and thank you kindly for the warmth of it."

"You'll be needing it yourself."

"Not a bit of it! With my gifts for the reading and the writing I'll be wearing silk within the month!"

"Tansy, are you going to stand there chattering until the boat turns around and goes back to Dublin?" Kate asked.

The hatches were being wrenched open and draughts of cold, dark air rushed down to the upturned faces, ruffling the ragged edges of shawls. The baby cried more loudly.

"God go with you," Tansy said swiftly to the fiddler, and Donal sketched a salute with his case, and turned, and was lost in the throng.

"Surely it's not a very decent thing," Kate said, "to be carrying on, and you not a week widowed."

"He was just a nice man to pass the time of day," Tansy said vaguely.

It was odd that Kate should be bothering about what was decent when there was so much else to fill their minds.

"Get a move on there! Watch that rope! Mind how you go! Will you stop shoving before you have half of us over the side! Look lively, you lazy Irish devil!"

Many voices, calling and cursing, merged into one voice amid a confusion of rocking timber, flares held high to point the narrow ridges of the gangway, faces straining onward as tired feet shuffled forward.

"There's a dead woman down there!"

"Shall we pitch her overboard?"

"And have the port authorities on my neck? Wait until I get down there."

"Now isn't it typical of an Irish biddy to go dying on board and not have the good manners to wait until we'd landed?"

Down the swaying, creaking gangplank they crawled like ants, clinging to the guideropes, with the wind blowing cold in their nostrils and the high hull of the ship behind them. All around them were echoing sheds and the windowless fronts of ugly, anonymous buildings.

"Soup!" Tansy paused, wrinkling her nose. "Kate, can you smell soup?"

"Over there!" Kate's thin hand pointed towards a row of trestle tables around which a crowd was swelling.

"Glory be to God! A soup kitchen!"

Tansy's spirits sprang up as she took Kate's arm.

But others had also smelled and seen, and a concerted rush began, as the column of human ants forgot the discipline of despair, and scattered, arms flailing, as they fought to reach the steaming cauldrons.

"We'll never get any," Kate said, her hand to her side. "We'll never get through the crowd."

"I can try," Tansy began, but she was elbowed aside by half a dozen women, who rammed their caps and shawls fiercely upon their heads and scrambled barefoot over the dark, wet stone.

"If I were bigger!" Tansy mourned.

Her lack of height had never troubled her very much, but combined now with the weakness of hunger it formed a barrier between her and the food.

"It isn't any use," Kate sobbed out hopelessly. "I told you it wouldn't be any use. We should have stayed in Ireland. Where's the sense in coming to England just to die?"

"We'll not die," Tansy pulled back her shoulders, fighting against the growing dizziness that threatened to drag her down into a swirling void. "I won't let us die!"

"Bravely spoken, colleen!" a voice approved. "If it's soup you're wanting, don't I know personally the good lady who's ladling it out? And won't I be there and back in a dragonfly's second to bring you both some?"

In the flickering light she could see only a thickset figure with a heavy gold chain glinting across a rose-sprigged waistcoat.

Then the man ducked away, weaving between the crowds as if he were a slender stripling. He was back almost at once with a mug in each hand, and a white grin splitting

16

the darkness.

"Drink up and then we'll be introducing ourselves!" he ordered.

The liquid was thick and hot, scalding her throat, sending warmth coursing to the ends of her fingers and toes.

"Not too quickly or you'll have the stomach cramps," he warned.

" 'Twould almost be worth it!" she retorted, draining the last drop. "You're a kind man, Mr. — ?"

"O'Leary, Malachy to my friends, of whom God and His Saints be praised I have more than my fair share!"

"I'm Tansy O'Faolain and this is my sister, Kate Malone."

"Married ladies?" His voice had chilled.

"Kate is single and my husband was hanged last week," she said flatly.

"Hanged? May God forgive the times we live in! But you'll have relations to meet you, no doubt?"

He was peering at her intently.

"There's nobody except Kate and me," Tansy said. "Nobody at all."

"Ah, God help the both of you! And you'll not have any lodgings then?"

"Liverpool is a big port," Kate said timidly. "We'd hoped to work our way."

"Seventy times seven Irish refugees land here with the same notion," he said sadly. "Most of them are packed forty to a room in the warehouses here."

"You seem to have done well enough for yourself," Tansy said.

"Ah well! I've got connections." He laid a thick finger

along the side of his nose and winked.

"Could you tell us how to find work?" Kate asked eagerly.

"What the both of you need at this moment in time," he said, "is a bed for the night and the chance of a good meal in the morning."

"And you know of such a place?"

"I *own* such a place! If you're ready, come with me."

He jerked his head towards the dark road that ran between the high, faceless buildings and the dockyards, and set off briskly, his boots ringing on the stone, his arms swinging short and powerful at his sides.

Over his shoulder he said, "Feast your eyes on the glories of the city! On your right the gaol; on your left the coal-tip. That's the Church of St. Nicholas — the Protestant St. Nick, of course! We turn here into Water Street, past Moorfields. Look ahead, colleens, and admire the fine new hall they're building in honour of St. George!"

The white stone gleamed against the dark sky. Tansy, tilting back her head, thought she had never seen such a grand building in her life. Its size and immobility frightened her.

"It's bigger than Devereux Place," she whispered.

"Where would that be?" He slowed his pace and waited for them to catch up.

"It was the great house where our landlord lived. When I was little, I used to sneak in and play there when the family was away. It was a big house with a staircase that curved around up to a gallery, but it would fit inside this place three or four times surely!"

"It's a marvellous tribute to the building skills of the

English," Malachy O'Leary said dryly. "Turn left here. It's not too weary a way now."

Tiredly they stumbled after him, passing others who, like themselves, toiled along the winding streets. Once, a small child shrilled after them.

"Mammy, mammy?"

"Mammy's probably dead to the world in an alley with a bottle clasped to her ever-loving bosom," Malachy said. He sounded more amused than otherwise.

"Is it a lodging-house you keep?" Tansy asked.

"It's a tavern, the prettiest tavern you can find this side of the Emerald Sea," he told her. "Ask anybody and they'll tell you that the *Black Boy* gives the fairest measure for miles around."

"The *Black Boy*? Is that the name of your tavern, Mr. O'Leary?" Kate enquired.

"Malachy to my friends, darling. And, yes, the tavern is mine since my poor wife, God rest her soul! passed away ten years ago. She was a widow-lady when I came over here, and a plumper little armful I never laid eyes on! But she died, poor soul, and left me the business. A kind of sacred trust, you might say."

"Profitable too?" Tansy asked innocently.

"Profitable enough." He gave her a sharp, searching look. "But I need help all the time in the bar and the cellars, and since my poor wife passed on, I've not had a meal cooked for me by a pretty woman. There's always room for willing hands."

"I can sew," Kate said. "I always did the mending at home."

"I can read and write," Tansy chimed in. "If it's a girl

19

to add up the takings you need —"

"A girl to add up the takings," he echoed, and was doubled up in a paroxysm of mirth, his arms folded across his chest, his broad shoulders quivering under the strained black broadcloth of his coat.

"I'm perfectly honest," Tansy said, indignation creeping into her voice. "You can ask Kate; or Father MacNabb, if you ever meet him."

"Whist! we're here," Malachy ordered, his laughter ceasing abruptly. "This is Grub Street just across from Shaw's Brow. And that's my tavern; but we'll slip in at the side door and up to the attic. It's cosy under the eaves and there's a big warm bed there for the two of you to snuggle up in like doves!"

Laughter and chatter and the flowing radiance of gas-jets spilled out into the street. Malachy turned into a narrow lane at the side of the building, and the girls were hemmed in at once by high walls and a smell so rank that Tansy's stomach heaved.

"The air is so thick in the city," Kate whispered.

"Surely, but you'll grow accustomed to it in less time than it takes to tell," Malachy informed her cheerfully. "Now if you'll be stepping this way, darlings, and be careful of the third step because it isn't there, I'll show you the room."

"About the mending," Kate began, but his voice over-rode them from the top of the steep, iron-railed staircase.

"God bless your willing heart but we can leave talk of the mending until the morning, if you'd be so kind!"

TWO

The room was small with a ceiling that sloped down over a large bed and a tiny window set high in the wall. Malachy fumbled with flint and lucifer, and the pale glow from a stub of candle lighted the wooden floor, the greyish walls, the tarnished brass knobs at the head and foot of the bed.

"It's hardly a palace," he said, curling his lip as if he had just realised the inadequacies of the place.

"It's a grand room!" Tansy felt warm gratitude rise up in her. "We never slept in a brass bed before."

"Ah, well, the sheets are clean, because I made the bed myself," he told her. "Now, be hopping between them and I'll be seeing you in the morning."

When he had gone the room seemed larger. Kate had moved to the bed and sank down upon it, her hands limp, her hair falling untidily over her shoulders.

After a moment she said hopefully, "He seems very kind, doesn't he?"

"Kind enough, though I'd like to know why he was hanging about down at the docks when it was past midnight and he has a business to run," Tansy said. "But if it means we have shelter and a real bed —"

21

"A soft one too!" Kate swung her legs round and stretched luxuriously.

"We'd best sleep and see what morning brings."

Tansy joined her sister and, heedless of her filthy, scratched legs and feet, burrowed deeply into the softness of feather mattress and thick blankets. A clock chimed somewhere, and in the street below faint sounds of argument and laughter drifted up to the tiny window. And then she was asleep, deeply and dreamlessly asleep, for the first time on English soil.

Rain woke her, drumming on the eaves, causing her, as she raised her head, to imagine she was at Perimara again, trapped in the little whitewashed cabin, with the potato plants black and rotting in the fields around, and beyond them the high walls of Devereux Place. But this was Liverpool, and Kate slept peacefully at her side, and the old country lay in the grip of famine across a tossing, turbulent sea.

A wave of dizziness assailed her as she slid her feet to the floor, and she was aware of a fierce and healthy hunger. The stub of candle had run into a pool of melted wax in its saucer on a little table by the door. Apart from the bed and the table there was no other furniture in the room.

Tansy opened the door and started down the steep and narrow staircase. It was broken in places, the third step, as Malachy had warned, being completely missing, and the plaster on the wall was of a sad dun shade, deeply cracked and scored with many names.

At the bottom a turn to the left brought her through a half door into an inner yard, stacked with crates and barrels, ankle-deep in the rain that fell relentlessly from the space of sky between the high walls.

"Over here! Kitchen door's open!" a woman's voice shouted.

Bending her head under the force of water, Tansy squelched across the drowned cobbles in the direction of the invitation. She was so cold when she arrived in the big, stone-flagged kitchen that her teeth chattered and her hair plastered to her neck and temples, felt like tendrils of ice.

"Bloody awful weather for August, isn't it?" the voice commented.

It came from a woman of ample proportions and indeterminate age who sat by a leaping fire, with her skirt turned back over her knees and a mob cap perched rakishly on dyed ginger curls.

"Is this still Mr. O'Leary's place?" Tansy asked shivering.

"Back end of it, dearie. You'll be one of the new girls."

"We landed from Dublin last night. Mr. O'Leary happened to be down at the docks and said he could offer us work."

"You'll be needing a wash," the woman said. "There's hot water in the kettle and the sink is through there. Soap and towels on the side. There's a dress for you to put on."

"Thank you. I'm Tansy O'Faolain, by the way."

Bridie had always insisted on a certain standard of politeness.

"Tansy — that's pretty. A pretty name for a pretty girl. You can call me Florrie."

The woman had a round, shiny face with deep pouches under blackcurrant eyes.

"Florrie," Tansy repeated obediently and went over to

the range where a big black kettle sang merrily.

Through the door indicated by the woman was a tiny stone pantry with a deep sink under a window across which a yellowed net curtain was neatly tacked. Soap and two thick towels were laid on the side and a dress of some green stuff hung on a hook behind the door.

Hunger pangs were muted in the bliss of hot water and foaming lather. Tansy stripped off the ragged remnants of her kirtle and surrendered to the luxury. Beneath the grime her skin was light honey, its contours scarcely discernible after months of fasting.

The dress was not new, though it was clean and warm and cheerfully hued. Bridie would have frowned at the low neck and short puffs of sleeve.

"Child, you've no hips and very poor excuses for breasts!" Florrie cried as Tansy emerged. "Malachy will have to feed you up speedily. There's breakfast ready for you. Sit down and eat it while I find a comb and dig these tangles out of your hair."

She had never seen such a breakfast in her life. Muffins dripped butter, honey lay coyly in its comb; bacon sizzled next to a rosy-hearted egg. The tea was fragrant and brown, and there was a dish of plums.

"Eat up now!" Florrie ordered again.

She had risen from her place and standing at the back of Tansy's chair, began to comb the mass of red-gold hair. The motion was brisk and soothing, the food was so tasty that it was hard to resist cramming it in one's mouth, and the woman's voice ran like a litany above the crackling of the fire.

"My, but you've nice hair! I never saw this colour on an

24

Irish girl before. And your sister — Malachy says she's fair too. Silver-blonde, he said."

"Kate! I'd forgotten about her. She'll be wondering where I am!" Tansy swung round guiltily, her mouth stuffed with bacon.

"Hold still, dearie!" Florrie exclaimed. "If your sister is awake, which I doubt, Susan will be taking up hot water and a clean gown and a morsel to eat, so you just fill your own inside and let me finish off my work."

"Who's Susan?" Tansy asked.

"She helps out," Florrie said vaguely. "Not too bright in the top storey is our Susan, but very willing."

"I thought Mr. O'Leary didn't have anybody to cook for him," Tansy frowned.

"Is that what he told you?" Florrie stood back and put her head on one side to observe her handiwork.

"Wasn't it true?"

"Half and half, dearie, like most of the tales he tells. I usually get the breakfasts ready as the girls come off their beat."

"Beat?" Tansy echoed in bewilderment.

"Night duties," Florrie substituted.

"Is there more than one girl, then?"

"Bless you, there are a dozen of them," Florrie said heartily. "Girl is a bit of flattery where some of them are concerned, if you ask me. Now I'm past forty — past nearly everything else, too — and I don't mind admitting it. I've got my little bit tucked away, and my own roof over my head, and Malachy sees me right, so who wants to be young? How old did you say you were, by the way?"

"I was sixteen in April. Kate is two years older."

"And you a widow already, but we won't dwell on such unpleasant matters. Live and let live I always — Annie, will you shut that door! The rain's coming in all over the step."

A girl with hair and gown plastered to her buxom shape had come in. Erupted, Tansy thought, might have been a better word, for the girl fairly flew into the centre of the kitchen where she planted herself, arms akimbo, and addressed a stream of complaints into the air.

"Never again, I do vow, will I take the Scottie road beat! A real lot of mean sods they are! And it started raining at four o'clock and everybody vanished into thin air. I've been pounding the pavements these past three hours with nowhere to go. It's not good enough and so I shall tell Malachy!"

"Tell me what?" a voice enquired from an inner door.

The tavern owner was shorter and broader in daylight than he had seemed in darkness, but there was the heaviness of power held in check in the set of his thick shoulders and the aggressive thrust of his clean-shaven jaw.

"It was cold and wet on the beat," Annie complained.

"Then you should have come home and waited until the rain eased off," Malachy said.

"Come back here when I'd not earned my night's lodging! I can just see the welcome waiting for me," Annie said scornfully.

She had a thin, bitter face and a flat, nasal twang in her voice that grated on the ear.

"As if I'd make one of my girls walk the streets for lack of a bed!" Malachy cried piously. "But you didn't really come back empty-handed, did you? You're a lot cleverer than that, Annie me darling!"

"I didn't get anything," Annie said sulkily.

"Ah, well, never mind," Malachy's large hand patted her wet shoulder. "Never mind. The *Saranak* is due in a day or two. You'd better take the dockroad beat and let May have Scottie road for a couple of weeks. Now be off and get dry!"

The girl gave him a long look in which mockery and defiance were oddly mingled, and flounced out. Florrie, at a barely perceptible nod from Malachy, went out too, and for a little space there was no noise except the crackling of the fire and the drumming of the rain.

Tansy drank the last of her tea and looked up to see his eyes fixed on her consideringly.

"Did you sleep well, me darling? Was it snug and warm for the pair of you?"

"Warm as straw on a winter's evening," she assured him. "I never slept in such a grand bed before. Indeed I never slept in a bed before if you really want to know."

"Surely that's not so, and you with the manners of a little lady!"

"Indeed it is and well you know it!" she flashed, half-amused, half-irritated. "You told me you needed help to run this place, but it seems you have plenty of helpers around here, and you don't need more!"

"God forgive your doubting nature," Malachy said sadly, "but I cannot blame you, knowing what a bad view of life experience has taught you. Couldn't it be just that I took pity last night on a couple of starving colleens —?"

"And brought us back to a bed that was already made up with sheets and blankets?"

27

"Where you slept soundly," he interrupted. "And now you sit, full of Florrie's beautiful cooking, and begin asking questions as if we were enemies. Now is that a fair way to treat me?"

"Perhaps it isn't," she said slowly, "and if there was only me, surely I wouldn't be minding. But there's Kate."

"Who is older than you."

"She's not strong," Tansy said defensively. "We've always taken special care of Kate. There were five of us, you see, and our parents dead, and only Granda to look after us. Bridie was the oldest and she brought us up as well as she could. It wasn't easy for her because Pat and Seamus drank all the time, and I used to sneak away and play in the big house and pretend I was a fine lady. But we all looked out for Kate because she wasn't strong."

"What became of your family?" he asked, pouring tea for himself and straddling a chair.

"Seamus and Molly — she was his wife — took the money we'd saved for the rent and went to Dublin. That was when the men came and burned the cabins, Michael's and ours. Michael was my husband. He was a quiet, respectable man and everybody said I was sensible to take him."

"What happened after the cabins were fired?"

"Granda died in the fire," she said in a low voice. "He wouldn't come out, you see, and a mattress fell across him and the smoke rose up and choked him. We made a hut on the river-bank and lived there through the rest of the winter and the spring. Bridie died; just gave up and died. Michael and Pat went to the big house to see if they could find anything that could be sold for food. The land agent was there and he shot Pat, and Michael hit out with his shillelagh and killed the land agent. His name was Keegan."

"And Michael was hanged, you said."

"In Dublin," she nodded. "He took some bits of silver to sell, but they had the Devereux crest on and so he was caught and hanged. Kate and I were to meet him there, but he was already dead while we were still on the road. Isn't that strange, that we should be walking all that way and Michael already dead?"

"So you took the boat?"

"We travelled free as ballast in the hold," Tansy said. "They told us there was work in Liverpool."

"And so there is," he said promptly, "for haven't I been offering you work since you arrived?"

"I'll not walk the dock road all night," she said. "I'll not come in cold and wet like —"

"Like Annie? Darling, there is no resemblance at all between you and that poor drab! Annie was born to pound a beat in Scottie road, but you can work indoors."

"Work at what?"

"In the bar," he said. "You're a bright little thing, and when you're fed properly you'll be pretty too. Now you could learn to draw ale and measure a tot of gin, and your sister —"

"Not Kate," she said swiftly. "Kate could never stand the noise and the long hours."

"Let Kate help about the house then," he shrugged. "It's a grand pity, for she's fine eyes and a delicate air, and she would have pulled in a better class of customer but there, if you won't have it you won't have it."

29

"Do we get paid?" she asked.

"Paid? Holy Mother of God, but do you think I'm a rich man! Haven't you seen how I scrape and save so that I can keep a good table for my girls. You'll get your board and lodging, the both of you, and a pretty pair of shoes and a shawl to match your dress. And the men give a few coppers if your face pleases them. You may keep half of what they slip you, and I'll look after the rest of it for you."

She was silent, twisting her hair around her finger in a half-forgotten, childhood gesture.

"Well, me darling, what's it to be?" he asked, exaggerating his brogue. "Is it to be the bar and a comfortable place in the city, or will you take your sister down to the warehouses and share fleas with all the others just landed from the Dublin boats?"

"It's to be the bar," she said at last, and the image of Bridie grew fainter in her mind.

"There's the sensible girl!" he approved. "You'll find the work easy enough when you're into the way of it, I promise you. And if you keep a cool head on your shoulders and a sweet smile on your mouth, sure you'll make a grand place for yourself in the world! Now come through to the front part and I'll show you the way of it."

The back regions were joined by a network of covered passages to the low-beamed room with the high bar cutting off a third of the space. Sawdust sprinkled the floor, high partitions divided each table and round-topped stool; beyond the small, grimed window panes the sign flapped wetly.

"This is Tansy O'Faolain," Malachy said, loud and

30

cheerful as if this were still some social occasion. "Tansy, this is Edward. He'll show you how to give fair measure and reckon the change and carry a full tray without spilling a drop. You need any help and Edward will look out for you."

From below the level of the grilled bar a shaggy head popped up and two deepset, reddish eyes frowned at her. They were set in the ugliest countenance that Tansy had ever seen, atop a powerful and shambling frame.

"She's small," Edward said at last.

In contrast to his appearance his voice was high and fluting. Yet it roused in Tansy no desire to laugh.

"She'll work well," Malachy told him. "You show her, Edward, how we do things."

He patted Tansy on the shoulder and went out, leaving her with the grotesque Edward who came round the grille with large hand outstretched and the glint of broken teeth making his grin more hideous.

"They call me Edward," he said. "Not Eddie. Never Eddie. Edward."

"I'll remember." She gave her hand shrinkingly into his huge grasp.

"Come back behind," he invited, "and I'll show you the way of it, and tell you the prices. We open up at twelve, close for an hour between five and six for a cleaning; open again till who knows when — depending on business. Some of the regulars have their own mugs, kept on the shelf here. You'll get to match names to faces. Anybody gives trouble and you call Edward. You give trouble and Edward comes anyway."

"I won't be giving any trouble," she promised hastily.

"You've no beat," Edward said.

"I told Malachy that I'd not take a beat. Not like Annie."

"And you say you'll cause no trouble." The reddish eyes twinkled suddenly.

"My sister and I — we only want to eat every day."

"Work and you will," Edward said.

It was, she decided, going to be harder than she had imagined. There were rows of bottles behind the grille, as well as dozens of pewter mugs, and a cupboard stacked with thick-rimmed tumblers. There was, she discovered, an art in the drawing of a tankard of beer with a good head on it. Her wrists were not yet strong enough to carry a laden tray with one hand, but Edward assured her that she would quickly get the way of it. He was setting himself out, she realised, to be helpful, and perhaps, in time, she would learn to regard him as a friend and not shudder away from his thick hands and high voice and pock-marked face.

Now and then, during the morning, girls wandered in, helped themselves to a drink, exchanged a few words with Edward, favoured Tansy with an inquisitive stare, and wandered out again. They wore cheap, brightly coloured wrappers soiled at neck and hem and flapping slippers trimmed with dyed fur, and even the younger ones had paint caked in the corners of their lips and their sleepy eyes.

Somewhere a clock chimed eleven, and Edward, interrupting Tansy in the counting of tankards, said. "One hour off now. Food in the kitchen is for the taking. Be sharp back, mind!"

The bar was clean and neat, the tables scoured, the

bottles marshalled in rows, the trays stacked. A mirror on the wall was polished so brightly that Tansy was hard put to it to tear herself away from her own reflection. The mirror was so much bigger than the one in Guffy's Bar had been, but her new green dress was almost the same shade as her Ceidlh dress. It had been as if the old and the new came briefly together and disintegrated into splinters of memory.

Kate was not in the kitchen, but a brief search revealed her in a small parlour that opened off one of the narrow corridors. She too had a new dress of grey and pink against which her hair shone faint silver.

"Are you busy, alanna?" Tansy asked, but it was obvious that, although Kate had a basket of mending at her side, her hands were idle, her mind strayed into space.

"This is a — a bad house," she said in a hurried, furtive whisper, motioning with her head that Tansy should close the door. "The girl, Susan, who helped me dress, told me that Malachy O'Leary and that woman called Florrie — this is a bad house, Tansy!"

"I know."

Tansy closed the door and joined her sister. The room was small and stuffy with heavy maroon drapes at the window and a vase covered with sea shells on the mantlepiece. Roses climbed up the wallpaper and there was rush matting on the floor.

"Bridie would die if she could see either of us in a place like this," Kate said with tears in her voice.

"Bridie is already dead," Tansy said flatly.

"It's not a place for respectable girls," Kate said

33

stubbornly.

"Place hasn't anything to do with it," Tansy argued. "Perimara was no place of sin, but that didn't stop Bridget O'Donavan from getting herself a bastard. It's what you are inside that counts, Kate. A bad girl will be a bad girl anywhere."

Her voice sounded wise and experienced, but inside her a child's voice still whispered. And what makes you think you're so good, Tansy O'Faolain? How do you know you won't walk down Annie's road and end up like Florrie?

Aloud, she said, coaxingly, "The work's none too hard, Kate. Sure I can do the serving and the washing in the bar without any trouble at all! And you can manage the mending and a bit of the cooking, can't you? I'll help you when I can, I promise. We can keep ourselves decent while we wait to get a place of our own. We'll have a place of our own one day."

"Malachy isn't going to pay us," Kate reminded her.

"But I can save up the tips I get in the bar," Tansy said eagerly. "Oh, Kate, this is better than starving, isn't it? We can have food and shelter and regular work, and it won't be for ever. It surely won't be for ever, Kate!"

Kate gave her a long silent look, then bent her head over her mending with every appearance of industry. Only her fingers shook slightly as if they resented the task to which she put them.

In the kitchen again Tansy munched a ham sandwich and drank two cups of strong and reviving tea from the big brown teapot. The hour was going too swiftly. Her head ached a little as if all the new people she had met were clamouring in her ears. It would have been pleasant to have gone back to the little attic room, and lie down on the brass bed, and pull the clean covers over her face, and sleep.

"Door's open, ducks!" Florrie said from the passageway. "Malachy doesn't like people who start late."

"I'm coming!"

Tansy swallowed the rest of her tea and stood up, surprised to find that her legs were shaking.

"They're not so bad," Florrie said with rough kindness, "if you keep a sharp tongue in your head and your wits about you."

But that had been a young Tansy with fewer than sixteen happy years to count off on her sun-browned fingers. That had been a confident Tansy who faced the little world of Perimara with a smile and a ready retort for the adults who sought to contain that world within a hedge of rules and regulations. This new Tansy with her borrowed gown and an attic room for her refuge was suddenly afraid.

"Edward will look after you," Florrie said. "No call to be afraid of any funny business where Edward is concerned."

"I see," said Tansy, without seeing anything at all, and she went through again into the bar.

The door was open now and a few customers had already drifted into the room. They were shabbily clad men with caps pulled low over their eyebrows and mufflers wound tightly about their necks. Rain dripped from the brims of their caps and their thick boots left footprints in the sawdust.

She stood for a moment, watching them, wishing

herself elsewhere. Then Edward turned his huge head towards her and called in his high voice.

"Three tots of rum wanted in the right-hand corner, lass. Step lively now!"

Taking a deep breath, she did as she was bidden.

THREE

Liverpool was the first city, apart from her brief glimpse of Dublin, that Tansy had seen. It towered above her, its buildings gaunt and stark against a sky perpetually darkened by smoke. At the same time it hemmed her in, its streets narrow, winding, repelling any hint of green. Its inhabitants moved quickly, not with a bright and running grace, but with a relentless and fixed purpose; that purpose being, she discovered, to make a living.

There had been very little money in Perimara, and, until the famine came, it hadn't mattered very much. In the city it was a crime to be poor. The poor lived in tenements, or crowded into the empty warehouses that sprawled along the river front. They gathered in the dockside taverns, and in the gaming halls, in the soup kitchens and the street markets, and talked in high, nasal voices, interspersed with varying brogues as more boats laden with human cargo landed at Victoria Dock.

Once a week, on Sunday mornings, Tansy and Kate walked, after Mass, up Copperas Hill, into the cleaner, paler air of the upper city. The streets were wider here, the buildings set behind wrought-iron gates at the end of

37

curving drives. There were trees and shrubs planted at intervals, and a constant stream of pony traps and carriages rolled past over the sloping cobbles. Families, returning from church to a Sunday dinner prepared by a fat cook, glanced incuriously at the two girls with shawls over their heads, and then fell to discussing the length of the sermon again.

"Did you ever see such pretty dresses before?" Kate asked, catching Tansy's arm as a four-in-hand went by, with two girls in pink velvet at the window.

There was a wistful note in her voice that held Tansy's attention. She had never heard Kate sigh for finery.

"They look like the Devereux girls," Kate said.

"Bad luck to them then," Tansy said briefly. "Our landlord and his family cleared out quickly enough as soon as the potatoes failed, and took all the pretty dresses with them, I'll be bound."

"If we only had some money!" Kate said.

"Enough for a pretty dress?"

"A dress that nobody ever wore before I put it on, and shoes with heels, and a bonnet with cherries under the brim."

"And a grand house in Raneleagh Gardens, with a black servant to open the door, and a handsome gentleman to help you into a shiny carriage?"

"What's wrong with wanting something?" Kate demanded.

"Nothing, but it's the getting it!" Tansy said, then seeing the petulant droop of her sister's lips, she exclaimed, "But you'll have all those things and more one day. Fine gowns, and a horse to ride, and a big house, and the gentleman too. You're so pretty, Kate, that someone will snap you up

38

soon."

"Bridie always feared I wasn't strong enough for marrying," Kate reminded her.

"Not for ordinary marrying, with the hard work and the washing and the squealing of babies in the night," Tansy agreed. "But a rich husband, Kate, why he wouldn't let his wife stir a finger. You could sit all day, do a little embroidery or arrange some flowers in a vase — won't that be something!"

"It would be Heaven," Kate said, and her eyes dreamed. "And you can come and live with me, and take care of my children, if I decide to have any. Would you like that?"

Tansy was silent, considering. They had reached the top of the hill now and could look down over the hazy city, softened by distance into a mass of blurred and gentle shapes. Below the houses the masts of ships in the harbour menaced the skyline. Her eyes flickered to them and rested there.

"Wouldn't you like a fine house?" Kate asked again.

"And what would I be doing in a fine house?" Tansy evaded. "When I was a little girl I used to think that nothing would be finer than to live at Devereux Place, because Perimara always seemed too small; and sometimes I wanted to run and run, right over the edge of the world. And then in Dublin I saw bigger houses, and here in Liverpool there are buildings that make Devereux Place look cramped. And none of the houses are big enough, because I'd always be wanting to walk out and see what lies beyond."

"You always did talk nonsense," Kate said tranquilly.

"If I'd been a man," Tansy said with fierce recklessness,

"I'd not have stayed on the land. I'd have put my belongings in a bag and tramped off to sail around the world. And not in the hold either, but upon the deck with the wind blowing."

"We have to get back. Malachy will be screaming for us," Kate said.

It was an exaggeration. Malachy O'Leary seldom raised his voice save in jest, but his presence hung over them like a shadow that might or might not engulf the sun.

Kate had the easier part with him. She never came into the bar, but stayed within the back regions where she occupied herself with the bits and pieces of domestic work that Florrie and Susan didn't do.

Malachy seldom came across her, and when he did he contented himself with a brief word and a pat on the shoulder, from both of which Kate shuddered away. Edward she had never even seen, for he didn't live on the premises, but came into the bar just after dawn and stayed until the last customer had been thrust out into the street.

"Let Malachy scream," Tansy said, but she began to retrace her steps.

As they descended from the broad to the narrow streets the tall masts sank from view and the air was smoky again, the carriages gone, the doors of the big houses shut fast behind the girls in their pretty dresses.

"Did you never want to leave Liverpool and sail away somewhere?" Tansy asked Edward during a lull that evening as they rinsed tankards.

"Where would I sail?" he asked.

"I don't know, Anywhere! China or the South Seas,

40

perhaps."

"Too hot; too many savages; too much rich food."

He ticked off reasons on his thick fingers.

"But did you never want to leave the city, to see other places?" she persisted.

"Why should I? I've my work here."

"But you can't just stay here until you die," Tansy argued.

"Good a place as any to die in," he returned stolidly.

"Not for me," she said defiantly.

"No . . . Not for you." He nodded his shaggy head. "I read it in your face the first time I saw you."

"Read what?" She had never pictured Edward in the role of fortune-teller.

"A wildness and a wishing," he told her. "My mother was Welsh and could lift the curtain of tomorrow. She did it with every soul she met; but I can only do it with a few."

"And what can you see for me?" she demanded.

"Just the wildness and the wishing and a moment when they'll come together; but that will be in another land, when you've shed your burden."

"What burden?"

He jerked his huge head in the direction of the inner quarters.

"That sister of yours," he said.

"Kate? Kate isn't a burden! Anyway, you don't know her," Tansy said indignantly.

"I've seen her, peeping sly and quiet around the door when I was behind the bar, and she didn't think I could see her," Edward said. "And Florrie told me —"

"Florrie is a spiteful old biddy!"

"That madam Kate sits by the fire most of the time declaring she's delicate and too much of a lady to work in the bar. Not too much of a lady to mind her sister working here though."

"Kate's my whole family," Tansy said. "She's all I have left of the Irish days. All the rest died, except for my brother Seamus. He went off somewhere, and we'll never see him again. Now there's only Kate."

"You're bringing the tears to my eyes," Edward said.

"Well, don't speak against Kate any more," she said irritably. "And I don't believe you can tell fortunes at all! A wildness and a wishing indeed! Now where's the sense of that?"

But in the early hours of the next morning, as Kate slept peacefully in the wide brass bed, Tansy stood on tip-toe to get a breath of air from the tiny window. October had come in, crisp and bright in the upper city, wreathed in fog around the dock area as if even the seasons favoured the rich. Her shoes were too thin and leaked water, and her gown was not substantial enough for winter. Three months had gone by and she was no nearer earning any money. Malachy told her that she ought to smile more at the customers, but it was hard to smile when her feet ached and her wrists throbbed with the constant fetching and carrying.

"If I could get away," she whispered to the grimed glass. "If I could get away somewhere and make some money; oh Mother of God! wouldn't I turn Kate into a fine lady then!"

It was cold in the attic now but when summer came again it would be stifling. Worse than both was the loneliness of spirit that gripped her. She had known it already in some measure when she had longed to be able to read and write. Father MacNabb had taught her how to do both, and little good they'd done her! In the *Black Boy*, apart from an occasional newspaper that Malachy jealously guarded for himself, there were only the labels on the bottles to read.

Kate stirred and muttered in her sleep, hunching deeper into the coverlets. Her arm, flung briefly out, gleamed thin and ivory. If anything happened to Kate —! Tansy shut down the thought and slipped into her place at the extreme edge of the bed where she could form a barrier between her sister and the draught from the door.

October blew into a dank November and the rain came again, slanting past wet roofs, and the high walls of St. George's Hall rising swiftly in the square from which streets radiated like the spokes of a broken wheel. Sunday morning walks were not too pleasant now. The carriages dashed past with their blinds drawn, splashing mud into the faces of pedestrians.

It was cold in the *Black Boy*, even though Florrie had the fires built high and gave the girls extra blankets. Susan caught cold and took to her bed, which meant that Kate had to do the rough work. She did it uncomplainingly, blackleading the grates, carting in the heavy buckets of coal, but her face grew pinched again and at night Tansy sometimes heard her crying quietly to herself.

"Make some money, dearie? Now why would you want to do that?" Florrie asked roguishly, when Tansy opened the subject.

They were together in the kitchen with the kettle singing on the hearth, creating an illusion of homeliness.

"Doesn't everybody want to make some money?" Tansy asked.

"You're not willing to work for it like the other girls though, are you?" Florrie cocked a gingerish eyebrow.

"Not like Annie and Maggie, no," Tansy said.

"Malachy gave you a good chance there." Florrie shook her head sadly. "It hurt his feelings when you turned up your nose."

"He got a couple of unpaid servants for all his hurt feelings," Tansy reminded her. "We don't cost him much in bed and board, and we're never off our feet. We work harder than Annie ever does, and she gets paid and keeps some of what she earns."

"If you won't go on the beat you'd better try rolling a sailor," Florrie advised. "But don't let Malachy catch you at it. He's no liking for the law breathing down his neck. The *Black Boy* had a good name."

"A better name than most. Nowhere around here has a good name!"

"Hark at Madam! Rescued from the bogs of Ireland and turns up her nose at honest Lancashire dirt," Florrie said and looked annoyed.

"We never lived in a — oh, never mind. Thanks for the advice." Tansy gulped the rest of her tea and went back into the bar.

The practice of rolling sailors, which had filled her with horrified amusement when she had first been told about it, was carried on in every quarter of the docks. The men, disembarking with jingling pockets, were easily persuaded to drink by the girls thronging the quays, and it was only slightly more difficult to relieve them of their money pouches as they lay helpless in the dark alleys.

Bridie would have killed me if she ever dreamed I'd have such a thought in my head, Tansy decided guiltily. But it's easy to be honest when you don't need any money.

That she had always been poor and never sunk to the contemplation of theft before was a detail she brushed aside. After all, her husband had been one of the most respectable men in the village, but famine had driven even Michael to steal. And led to his being hanged!

She glanced anxiously towards Edward, wondering if he could be persuaded to let her leave early. If she were going to do it, it would have to be tonight.

"Holy Mother, but I'm weary!"

One eye on the clock, she sagged against the bar, cloth dripping limply from her hand.

"You look a bit pale," Edward allowed. "Would you like to slip off for an hour, put your feet up?"

"Can you manage without me?"

"I managed before you came, so an hour or two won't hurt me now. Don't go thinking I rely on you for anything!"

"I won't," she promised.

"Be back at twelve. The *Saranak*'s in, and we'll be packed out by then," he warned her brusquely. "If Malachy sees you, tell him I've sent you on an errand."

"I'll do that and — thanks."

She feigned a yawn and remembered to walk slowly to the door. Once in the street, however, she took to her heels and flew over the cobbles, cutting in and out of the alleys as if she had been bred among stones instead of in green fields.

Here and there gas jets flared briefly in the yellow mist

rising from the river, but for the most part the streets were dark. Voices, distorted by the fog, came faintly as if from a great distance and the acrid smell of tar teased her nostrils.

She wrapped her shawl more tightly about her head and went forward slowly, one hand outstretched to warn herself of the projecting corners of buildings.

A light drizzle of rain sprayed her face, and she stood for a few moments with uplifted head, catching cool drops on her tongue and lips, letting her eyes grow accustomed to the murk. A halo of dim yellow light circled her head, glinting on the tendrils of red-gold hair that curled damply on her temples.

The young man approaching her stopped for a moment, drawing in his breath slightly as if he doubted whether she were quite real. She stood so still, her lips parted to catch the rain, her shawl slipping from her head.

Then his foot struck against a cobblestone and she lowered her head to peer into the gloom that surrounded her. Taken unaware she had a startled faunlike air, as if she were poised on the edge of flight.

"I'm sorry if I startled you, ma'am. I guess I was so busy just plain admiring you that I forgot my manners."

The voice was flat and slightly nasal. It issued from a stockily built young man whose features, from what she could discern in the half-light, were broad and fair, marred by a long chin.

He thrust the chin forward now as he said, "I'd be obliged if you could direct me to an eating-house. This is only my second trip to Liverpool and I'm kind of a green-horn around here."

He wondered if she were slightly deaf or slightly deficient for she went on staring at him with her mouth open. In fact she was so astonished at the ease with which a sailor — and an officer from the look of him — had fallen into her clutches that she hadn't the faintest idea what to say.

"Do you know any such place, ma'am?" he repeated patiently.

"Tansy. My name is Tansy," she pulled herself together briskly. "And yes, I can show you a grand place to eat."

Jenny's Chophouse in Byrom Street was a warm and friendly little place, more expensive than most because it was more respectable. It had separate tables with lamps on where the customers could sit, and the girl who waited on was clean and polite.

"My name is Jan Harrow, Miss Tansy, if I may introduce myself," He gave a stiff little bow. "Perhaps you'd do me the honour of joining me?"

He gave her a doubtful look as he spoke.

At twenty-four, Jan Harrow considered himself to be a man of the world. He was well aware that respectable girls didn't roam about the waterfront at night, but this Tansy girl lacked the paint and feathers of the typical dockside harlot. Her dress was bright and low-cut but decently covered by a shawl, and there was a cleanliness about her that reminded him of his grandmother's kitchen.

"I'd be pleased to join you," She felt suddenly shy as if this were a real social occasion.

They turned and walked back, each aware of the other, carefully not touching. He volunteered the information that he was off the *Saranak*, a detail she had already guessed.

47

"My regular ship is the *Marybelle* but they have an exchange of officers sometimes between British and American craft, to study different methods of navigation."

"It sounds very interesting," she said politely.

"It's a good life. The truth is that my folks just didn't know what to do with me after I made it clear I wasn't interested in the family's store."

So his family had a store.

"Is it," she enquired, "in New York?"

"In Boston. My parents still live there, though we're originally from Pennsylvania. Dutch."

"I thought Dutch people lived in Holland," Tansy said, surprised.

"My great grandparents came over from Zeeland. Their name was Hartog but my grandfather changed it to Harrow. My grandmother still likes to speak Dutch when she can. You're Irish, aren't you?"

"We came over after the crops failed," she began.

"The famine." He nodded sympathetically. "My great-grandparents went to America after their home was flooded. The whole town sank under the sea."

She pictured streets and houses sinking slowly under a weight of water and the people running away, growing smaller and smaller in the distance. It seemed to her that the whole world was continually on the move, forever running from one fear to another fear.

They had reached Byrom Street and the lamps at each side of Jenny's Chophouse glowed a welcome. One of the local whores glided forward but, seeing the man was already accompanied, gave a good-humoured shrug and melted into the shadows again.

They found a corner table and sat down. The place was only half-full and Joan, raising an inquisitive eyebrow at Tansy, took the order promptly. When the laden plates of steak and baked potatoes arrived, a silence fell. Jan Harrow's healthy appetite had been frustrated during the voyage by the officers' food which was only slightly less unappetising than the men's. Now he tucked in heartily, wielding his knife and fork like weapons before which the defenceless meat fell into succulent pieces.

Three months of regular meals had sheared the edge of Tansy's hunger. There had been a time in Ireland when she would have torn at the meat with her fingers. Now she set out to eat daintily while she racked her brains for something witty and clever to say. Nothing occurred to her, however, so she contented herself with an occasional smile across the table at her partner.

"That was real good!" He wiped his mouth with the paper napkin next to his elbow and reached for the carafe of red biddy that Joan had brought.

Tansy's heart sank a little. The pleasant part of the evening was over. Now, if she were to carry out her original plan, Jan Harrow must be encouraged to drink more and more until he lost all sense of balance, and could be relieved of his money, and shoved aside in order that she might make good her escape.

The trouble was that she was beginning to feel less and less inclined to cheat and rob the stocky, blunt-faced young man who leaned towards her and began to talk pleasantly. He was neither handsome nor amusing, but there was a frankness in his bearing that attracted her. He was talking about his family, telling her about his father, who had wished his only son to follow him in the business the great-grandfather had built up, but had had the wisdom to let the boy choose his own way.

"My mother is of British origin, I get my long chin from her side of the family. My two sisters escaped it. Gerda is really pretty. Sigrid is the clever one. You'd like them both, I guess."

"I had two sisters," Tansy said.

A wistful note in his voice struck an answering chord in her own heart, and suddenly she was telling him about Bridie who had been the strongest in the family and yet had lost hope and died; and Kate who was so frail and yet had survived.

"So you left Ireland and came over to Liverpool. That was real spunky!" he admired.

"There wasn't anything else to do," she said honestly. "We'd have starved if we'd stayed in Dublin."

"But how do you earn a living here?" he asked, and blushed to the roots of his cropped fair hair at the tactlessness of his enquiry.

"We work at the *Black Boy* — that's a tavern in Grub Street. I help in the bar and Kate helps with the housework. We get food and shelter, so it's not so bad."

A conscious note of brave endurance crept into her voice.

"It doesn't sound much of a job for a girl like you," he said.

"Oh, it's not so bad," she said fairly. "There are so many Irish over here now that we were lucky to get anything at all. And Malachy leaves us fairly free, provided the work gets done."

"You said your husband died." His glance had roved to the tarnished band on her finger.

"He was hanged for stealing," she said briefly. "Not that Michael was a thief, you understand. But when times are hard —"

She spread her small calloused palms wide and let her shoulders droop in defeat.

"It's a hard world." He frowned slightly as if he were passing judgement on the world. "But we have to live in it."

She eyed the red biddy, noting that, though the level in the carafe had sunk appreciably, his eyes remained clear, his speech unslurred. She had heard somewhere that the Dutch could drink a lot without being affected. It looked as if Jan Harrow, for all his schoolboy innocence, had inherited the hard head of his ancestors.

"I guess I'd better walk you back," he said at last.

There was a certain reluctance in his voice. Close to, in lamplight, the girl was enchanting. He wanted to reach out and touch her hair, but the shyness bred in him by a strict upbringing stayed his hand.

"It's not far from here," she told him, and there was a reluctance in her face too. She had no desire to let him see Malachy's tavern where the customers would already have begun singing and squabbling, and Annie and Maggie would be moving among them with avid eyes and greedy fingers.

And I, she thought guiltily, am no better. At least Annie gives a little pleasure in return for her money. I wasn't even willing to do that.

He had taken a pile of coins from an inner pocket and was sprinkling them on the table with a reckless abandon that made her want to weep.

"Would it be — would you permit me to call on you some time when we're next in port?" he was asking.

"If it's a Sunday," she said, a little breathless with disappointment now that her plan was finally given up, "we usually walk up to Raneleagh Gardens after Mass. There are trees up there and seats to sit on."

"Next time I'm on this run then."

He gave his stiff little bow, deciding not to offer the money he had originally intended to give. The girl might be hurt at the suggestion that he was paying for her company. He supposed that he ought to set about finding a woman for the night, but when Tansy had gone, he ordered another carafe of red biddy, and sat staring dreamily into a green land.

FOUR

"You've a long face on you this morning," Edward said. "Don't you like Christmas then?"

"Not when it's cold and slushy and the water freezes in the jugs," Tansy said crossly.

"Take the afternoon off and do some shopping," he offered.

"With what?"

"You've some money owing to you. Tips from people. Some of them gave it to me to keep for you."

"I didn't know that." She gave him a disbelieving look.

"I was saving it for a surprise." he said blandly.

"How much?"

"A guinea," he said.

"A guinea!" Now she was certain he was lying. "Who in Liverpool would go throwing away a guinea on a bar-room girl?"

"Bits and pieces," Edward said vaguely, "mount up. I changed them into a guinea for you. Don't spend it all at once."

"No. of course not." She blinked at the shiny coin.

"Then what are you waiting about for?" he demanded.

"I'm not, I'm not. I'm going!" She grabbed her shawl and unwound the stained apron from her waist.

The cold wind blowing down the street made her hesitate for a moment, and then she was trudging resolutely through the ankle-deep slush. It had been trampled by countless feet into an ugly criss-cross pattern of lines and whorls, but in the corners and crevices of the buildings it was still white and every window bore a delicate fingering of frost.

Tansy could not remember having seen snow in Ireland and the whiteness of the world suddenly enchanted her. A lad selling hot baked potatoes at the corner of New Scotland Road and Dryden Street sang his wares in a raucous voice, and a little flurry of snow whipped free from an overhanging cornice and scattered benediction on his head. He looked so comical, standing there with his cloth cap dripping white flakes, that Tansy began to laugh.

Still laughing she crossed the road and went up Dryden Street, her thin soled shoes crunching the ice. There were shops here; small, respectable shops, each with its own sign and character. The pharmacy with its squat green bottles and bunches of thyme and marjoram usually pleased her. So did the gown shop with its swathes of coloured silk and velvet; its headless, legless dummy, its bunches of artificial flowers and lengths of taffety ribbon. Today, however, she wasted no time on window-gazing, even if the windows were decorated with ivy and holly leaves and bows of scarlet ribbon. Today she owned a guinea, and she knew exactly what she was going to buy with it.

At the top of the street, just before it joined Great

Homer Street was the little, dark façade of the millinery shop. It was pressed between two larger shops that looked as if they were trying to elbow it out of their company, so confined did the small bow window and the narrow doorway seem.

There were never more than two or three bonnets perched on iron stands to be glimpsed through the dim glass, and the fact that they were ever changed at all puzzled Tansy, for the little bell that hung over the front door was rusty with disuse.

Above the door faded gold lettering proclaimed Rosa Schindler, Milliner, but as a screen at the back of the window bay cut off the interior, it was impossible to hazard a guess at the appearance of the lady.

Today the shop bore neither holly wreath nor scarlet bow, and wedged between its gaily decorated neighbours, looked faintly ashamed of itself as if it would have liked to take a step backwards and cease to intrude.

Tansy's eyes flew at once to the window and stayed there, riveted in relief on the creamy little bonnet with its bunch of red cherries under the fluted brim. It had not been sold or exchanged for some less tempting creation. It was still where she had first seen it a month before, its ribbons dangling limply, its round fruit glowing rosily in their nest of green leaves. She had thought about the bonnet ever since her first glimpse of it, and never thought about it without seeing Kate's tranquil face under the frivolous brim.

Kate hadn't seen it yet for she seldom ventured into town except on Sundays, but when she did see it — when she did see it, Tansy thought, colour would rise under her pale skin and her grey eyes would shine.

The picture of Kate's delighted face sent Tansy up the two shallow steps and through the panelled door into the shop. There were hats piled on a shelf below a long mirror, and two chairs close to a flap-topped counter.

As she entered, the bell over the door gave an alarmed squawk. There was nobody in the shop and, for a moment, she stood still, her eyes feasting on the glowing colours of the bonnets, her ears attuned to the dim echoing of the bell, her nostrils twitching as the mingled mustiness of dust and camphor assailed them.

For Tansy every place had its own smell and sound and colour and over and above that some atmosphere stamped upon it by the events that had happened there. In her memory, where recent happenings were blurred by the pain of them, Perimara was still green peat singing high and clear in the joy of small, familiar things. Liverpool was grey smoke carried by the wind across the black river and the steady tramping of feet on hard pavements. Despite the pretty bonnets, this little shop was brown dust sighing.

"May I help you?"

The voice sounded vaguely surprised as if its owner doubted very much if he were capable of helping anybody. Turning to look at him, Tansy inwardly agreed. He was old, past sixty, with scraps of grey hair hanging about a lined, yellowish face. For an instant she even felt a stab of fear, but it was gone as he smiled at her and came closer to the other side of the counter. There was sheer good-humour in that smile and a twinkling fellowship in those pouched eyes.

"You're not," Tansy said, "Rosa Schindler."

56

"My wife. She has been gone from me these past three years."

His smile had hardly wavered but the air was suddenly full of sadness so keen that her own eyes filled.

"Mr. Schindler?" she questioned.

"Conrad Schindler."

He gave her a little bow with his hands spread wide as if he were apologising and shrugged bent shoulders in a gesture that was un-English; and his speech was, she noticed, also faintly accented as if he had learned the tongue late in life.

"Are you Dutch?" she asked, her mind jumping back to the young sailor whom she had failed to rob. She had not seen him since that night but the remembrance of his kindness warmed her.

"German," he corrected. "I came to this country with my wife when I was twenty-three years old."

"Was there a flood?" she enquired with interest.

"There was a pogram," he began, and seeing her puzzled expression amended it to, "There was much ill-feeling against the people of my race, against the Jews. Many died or were killed. Many more fled."

"We fled the famine," she nodded.

"You are from Ireland then." His old eyes pitied her.

"There are thousands of us here now," she informed him. "My sister and I are the only ones of our family left."

"You lost your husband too, as I lost my Rosa?"

He was looking at her chapped hand with the greenish ring.

"Michael is dead too," she said, but there was no real sadness in her tone. She had never loved Michael nor

57

grieved for him more than she would grieve for a dear friend, and it was getting harder to remember exactly what his face had looked like.

"That is a tragedy for so young a girl."

He placed the tips of his fingers together and gave her an enquiring look, as if his mind was moving slowly back to the possible reasons for her being in his shop.

"You have a bonnet in the window," she was reminded to say. "A cream one with red cherries and green ribbons."

"You wish to see it?"

At her eager nod he shuffled over to the screen and twisted his lean frame around it to hook out the bonnet.

"The ribbons will not match your gown," he pointed out. "They are a much darker shade."

"It's not for me," she explained. "It's for Kate."

"For your sister?"

"It's a Christmas present," she said. "Kate is very fair, with grey eyes, and a pale skin. The bonnet will look grand, won't it?"

"Very grand. My Rosa fashioned it herself while she was ill. Only now do I bring myself to put it for sale."

His long hands stroked the velvet as if it were a woman's hair.

"How much would you be wanting for it?" she asked.

"The bonnet is expensive material," he said.

"But not in the very latest fashion," Tansy retorted.

"And of great sentimental value," he said, and drew the ribbon delicately between finger and thumb.

"I have a guinea." She was weary of bargaining before it had begun.

"In the big shops in London such a bonnet would fetch

five pounds!" he explained.

"Then it's too expensive," she said sadly.

"I have others that are cheaper," he said, but she shook her head.

"Kate wanted cherries," she told him.

"If you wished to pay for it a little at a time," he suggested.

"That's no use either. I don't get any wages, you see. The guinea is from the bits people give me after I've served them, though I think Edward put most of it there himself."

"Edward? Who is this Edward?"

"He keeps the bar at Malachy's place, at the *Black Boy*. Malachy O'Leary owns the tavern and I help Edward in the bar. Kate keeps house and Susan helps her."

"But surely you are paid for the work you do!"

"We get our board and keep and some time off for ourselves," she explained. "It really isn't too bad, but we do need a little money."

"For bonnets with cherries on?"

He looked again at her reddened hands, their tips white-swollen and weeping.

"Kate isn't strong," she explained patiently. "Even when I was a small child I knew she wasn't as hardy as the rest of us. It's a miracle she was spared in the family. But the city is harsh and she isn't happy, though she never speaks of it."

"A guinea would buy a pair of woollen stockings and a muffler," he said.

"Oh, Kate doesn't go out much in the cold weather," she assured him. "Her duties are in the house, you see. And even if they weren't, a bonnet with cherries on would lift

59

up her spirits far more than woollen stockings."

He frowned for a long moment as if he were trying to read her mind behind her face. Then he said abruptly, in his precise, accented English, "This *Black Boy* is not, I think, a respectable place for a young girl to be."

"Not exactly respectable," she admitted. "But it's not the place that makes a body respectable, is it?"

"And that is what my Rosa would have said! Almost could I sell you the bonnet for one guinea, but my Rosa would have then said I was a bad businessman, for tomorrow a rich lady might look in my window and offer me double the price for it."

He spoke with such ringing conviction that Tansy couldn't bring herself to ask him how many rich ladies had strayed in the direction of his small shop recently.

"So that's it then," she said, and even managed a shaky little smile as she bobbed a curtsey.

The combination of heartache and gallantry proved the final straw. Rosa had been a good business woman, but she would not have been able to stand against this appealing child with the big honey-coloured eyes and the cloud of red-gold hair. Almost against his conscious volition he heard himself speaking.

"You might like to pay the difference in labour. I live now, since my Rosa went, at the back of the shop. This is not my only concern. I tutor in German also. Privately. There are two rooms above the shop. They are much neglected now and never used. If I could find somebody to occupy them, and to serve in my shop —"

He stopped, appalled, for the very last things he needed were two penniless Irish girls from the dock area to clutter up his house.

"I couldn't pay you," he finished hastily.

"Glory be to God! but you ought not to bother your head about that!" she exclaimed. "Why, we'll make the place just as neat and decent as you can imagine. Kate can serve in the shop. She can try the hats on herself and she'll look so pretty that all the ladies will buy them so that they can look pretty too! And there'll be no trouble about my meals for I can still work at Malachy's and get them there, and come back here at night. Surely it's a beautiful idea!"

Her whole face was transfigured, so flushed and shining with delight that for an instant the sadness of the room lifted.

"You would be advised to see the rooms first," he said hastily, before the tide of joy flowing from her could drown his caution.

"Surely I will!"

She followed him eagerly, her young footsteps hastening his slower pace, through the curtained archway behind, and up a flight of narrow steps. Two rooms led one out of the other at the top of them. They were small and both cold and stuffy, but the outer room held a table and two chairs, a sofa, and piles of books overspilling a high bookcase and ranged in heaps round the edge of a worn carpet.

"I was," said Conrad Schindler, "a great reader in my time."

"I never saw so many in one room before!" Tansy gasped "At Devereux Place in Ireland, where our landlord lived, there was a library; but the books were all the same colour and never looked as if anyone ever pulled the poor things from their shelves."

"You can read?"

"Father MacNabb taught me the reading and the writing himself," she said, as unconscious of the implied insult in his comment as he was. "You might not be knowing it, but in our Faith a priest is a most educated man."

"All faiths are the same to me," he told her. "None of them bring any comfort in the end."

She had a vague feeling that the meaning of faith was not human consolation, but the feeling could not be translated into words that she could understand, and she was too interested in the books to rack her brains over obscurities.

"May I read these? All of these?" she asked shyly.

"The German ones and those in Greek and Hebrew will be of no use to you; but some of the others may give you pleasure," he said cautiously.

"Fairy tales?"

She picked up a volume and looked at it in surprise. She had never heard of tales of the little folk being written down before.

"They were Rebecca's," he said, taking the volume from her hand and caressing it as he had caressed the bonnet.

"Was Rebecca your little girl?" she asked.

"Our only one."

"And she died?"

There was that in his face which told her that Rebecca had not lived to grow up and read fairy stories to children of her own.

"She passed on when she was ten years old," he said.

'Died' was a word that he seemed to avoid, as if his loss of faith had brought with it such a fear of dissolution that all mention of it must be disguised in phrases that cloaked the real meaning of the event.

"I'll take good care of the book," she said, and, taking it from his hand, laid it back on the pile, with a precise, finicky little gesture which reminded him so much of Rebecca that he was startled.

"There are two beds and a cupboard in the next room," he said, to ease the moment. "It is all very dusty, you see."

"Dust can be wiped away," she said cheerfully, and ran to the window, breathing hard upon the rimed glass.

"I can see the trees in a garden from here!" she cried a moment later.

They were no more now than the bones of trees weighed down with snow, but in the spring they would be green for a little while until the soot blackened them again.

"The chimneys need sweeping and I cannot waste money on a boy," he said.

"I can clean the worst of them myself," she insisted. "May we come here at once? Today? I can begin now to make it ready."

"You had better talk about it with your sister first," he said, alarmed.

"Kate likes what I like and she will love it here," she told him. "Do you have any beeswax and old cloths and a stiff brush and a pail of hot water?"

"In the cupboard somewhere, I believe."

He looked about him in bewilderment, but she was galvanised into activity as if she feared the little rooms would vanish as soon as she stood still. In a daze Conrad Schindler found himself, under her enthusiastic direction, heating up water, hunting out the polishing cloths and the stiff broom that Rosa had wielded to such good effect.

Tansy had taken off her shawl, and with one of Rosa's aprons tied twice around her waist, was swishing about energetically. Sometimes she hummed under her breath, partly to express her delight in the unexpected turn of events, partly to hide the exquisite agony of chilblained fingers plunged into near-boiling soapy water.

It was mid-afternoon when she had finished, and only then did she realise that her back ached and she was ravenously hungry. But the rooms were ready. Hot water had cleaned the windows and the brown paintwork, stiff brushes had removed fluff and dust from the carpets and chimneys. She had leaded the little hearths, and laid wood, paper, and coal from a small stock in the back yard. The books were ranged in neat piles on the shelves and floor, and a gingham cloth covered the scratched surface of the table. From the cupboard she had pulled sheets and blankets that were only slightly motheaten and a spare length of gingham had been cut up and hung, still unhemmed, at the window.

Spurred by her efforts, Conrad Schindler had dug out some crockery and cutlery, a highly coloured print of a Spanish lady with castenets, and a mirror with a gilded frame of leaves and several squint-eyed Cupids.

Laying the table, hanging the Spanish lady over the fireplace where she could be reflected in the mirror opposite, Tansy thought of Michael. His face was already dim, for her affection for him had never grown beyond liking, but he would have enjoyed this room. It seemed a pity that her husband could not have seen such a grand place, that he had known only the bleakness of the cabin at Perimara.

Yet mingled with her regret was a certain relief. He would never have been able to make his way in the city, nor meet others on equal terms, for he had been, she thought with compassion, a limited man. Even the books would have been quite useless, for he had never understood the need that was in her to learn the reading and the writing so that her small world might be enriched and opened up.

"I have made coffee and there are rolls warming in the oven," Conrad Schindler said, coming in.

She would have liked to invite him to sit down at the table, but the first meal in their new home must be reserved for Kate, so she went with him down to the room at the back where he set out mugs of bitter coffee and rolls that had scorched a little at the edges.

As he poured the coffee she noticed that the end of his coat sleeve was frayed and his cravat was torn. It must, she thought, be hard for a man to lose his mate, yet it irritated her that he should let himself go in such a fashion. It was little wonder that so few customers came into the shop. The bell had not sounded once since her arrival.

"I will go back and tell Malachy that Kate is leaving," she said. "And Kate and I will come as soon as I have finished my work tonight. Do you have a spare key, for it will be past midnight when we have finished."

"There is Rosa's key," he said and was surprised at himself, for it was a long time since he had trusted either God or man.

The big iron key that had hung at Rosa's wide waist, with her smaller keys to pantry and store cupboard, lay now in the top drawer of the dresser. He detached it from its ring and gave it to Tansy with solemnity. She, unconscious of ritual, tucked it briskly down the front of her dress and reached for her shawl.

"Kate will be so happy here," she said. "She will keep everything bright and more people will come into your shop. It will work out so grandly, you'll see!"

"What of the bonnet?" he enquired.

"I hung it on the bedpost," she told him. "Tonight, when we come here, it will be waiting for her."

"And the guinea?"

He had no intention of giving the bonnet away, despite her charm.

"I have it here, Mr. Schindler." As she handed over the coin, she exclaimed, "Glory be to God! You don't even know my name!"

He had not thought of enquiring it, for in his mind she moved and talked as Rebecca.

"I'm Tansy Malone O'Faolain." She gave each word its due importance. "I am called Tansy by most people. The tansy-flower is a yellow bloom that grows wild in our hedgerows. When my grandmother was wed she wore some in her hair. Her name was Kathleen and Kate was named after her, but I was named for the flowers she wore."

"Tansy," he repeated obediently, and thought privately it was a ridiculous name. Yet his own wife had been named for a flower, though a brisk, no-nonsense blossom she had been. At times he had resented her domination, but since her death he could remember only her cheerful voice and the smell of her baking. He was apt to be melancholy himself, and to forget to eat until he began to feel faint and dizzy.

Rebecca had often teased him about it, but her teasing

had been gentle. A good, gentle child, he mused, and railed once again at the God whom he no longer trusted for having sent the doom of cholera down upon her innocent head. After her death he had never gone to the synagogue again despite Rosa's pleading. In all matters, save this one, her will had been supreme, but this had made a little breach between them that lasted until her own death.

The untidy kitchen was still and shadowy again. The Tansy-girl had gone and, for an instant, he felt the clutch of panic lest she had helped herself to anything on the way. The pile of coppers in the tin on the mantelshelf was undiminished, however, and the guinea glinted on the table. It seemed that she was as honest as she looked, though he reminded himself firmly that it would be foolish to jump to any firm conclusions.

In the street Tansy was walking slowly away. Her whole being wanted to dance and sing, but the ice made the road treacherous and there was, moreover, so much delight within her that she wanted to hug the pleasure of it to herself for a little while.

Only bad news, she reflected, should be quickly told. Good news should be savoured and then let out a little at a time. And this was good news, so good that she felt a trifle breathless when she thought about it.

As for Malachy O'Leary! When she thought of him her mind took a defiant stand. After all, there was Florrie and Susan to do the work, and she would still be there herself to serve in the bar. Malachy had no reason to complain.

By springtime Kate and she would be settled in their little home and the shop would prosper. Tansy knew it in her bones. In springtime, too, the trees in Raneleagh Gardens would put forth their leaves, and she and Kate would walk there after Mass on Sundays.

The thought of Jan Harrow was another pleasure. Surely he would come back when the opportunity arose, and she could tell him of her altered circumstances, and introduce him to Kate. The three of them might even become friends. They were all exiles of a kind, even Mr. Schindler; and her plans widened a little to include the shopkeeper in the circle.

FIVE

Christmas had come and gone into a cold January, and January had dwindled into a damp February. The snow had melted into grey puddles along the gutters, falling in soft exhaustion from the eaves of the houses.

The shop in Dryden Street bore the same crushed and desolate appearance as it had worn when Tansy first saw it, but the two rooms upstairs had a comfortable, lived-in look. Kate kept them warm and clean, taking great pride in the polishing and dusting. Tansy brought home sprays of evergreen and bits of coloured stone she had found along the foreshore, and decorated the window-sills and mantelshelves, her taste leaning towards the brightly exotic.

She still worked at the *Black Boy* and took her two meals of the day in the kitchen with Florrie. Malachy had been none too pleased at the news that they were leaving, but as he had never paid them, there was nothing he could do.

Another girl, a redhead from Donegal, had replaced Kate, and from the looks of her, Tansy suspected it would not be long before she joined Annie on the beat. Edward, when she asked him, said briefly that Eileen was a trollop and that she and Kate were lucky to be out of it, but he worked her as hard as ever in the bar so that sometimes she could scarcely lift her feet for weariness as she trailed home.

Kate was usually in bed and asleep and she seldom woke up before Tansy left in the morning, so there were few opportunities for conversation, but her pale face bore a serene, contented look, and her exclamations of delight over the bonnet had been as fervent as her sister could have wished.

Life had fallen into a neat, well-ordered pattern. Tansy went off to the *Black Boy* at eight each morning and, apart from a couple of hours off for her meals, stayed until midnight. She was growing accustomed to the hard work now. Her wrists were like steel and she could twist between the tables like lightning when one of the men made a grab for her, but she could never grow accustomed to the noise and smoke, to the harsh, nasal accent of the men who teased and propositioned her, to the hard pavements under her thin soles, and the bitter wind that swept across the river.

Worse than those was the loneliness of spirit that gripped her sometimes. It had happened occasionally in her childhood when she had heard the other little girls talking of when they would be married with babies, and she had known deep down that she didn't want to spend the rest of her life in Perimara. But at least her village had been a safe, familiar place. In this English city there was precious little safety, and the people one passed in the street had different faces every day.

Her loneliness was eased a little on the occasions when she could get to the docks and watch the big ships glide in accompanied by their fussy little tugboats. The swell of their sails lifted her heart, and the brown-faced boys with gold hoops in their ears who swarmed about the rigging filled her with a desire for something she could not understand that seemed to lie perpetually just beyond her reach.

Sometimes she remembered what Edward had said of her. A wildness and a wishing that would come together in another land when she had shed her burden. The words excited her even while they made no sense.

"What you need is a man," Florrie told her one day, when she had found Tansy staring dreamily into the yard, a cold mug of tea in one hand and a half-eaten biscuit in the other.

"What would I be doing with a man?" she asked indifferently.

"How old are you?"

"Seventeen in April."

"Then you're old enough to answer the question yourself," Florrie told her with a loud cackle of laughter. "Anyway you've had a husband, haven't you? Don't you miss having a man in your bed?"

Tansy screwed up her nose as she considered the question. Michael had been gentle and kind, but she had never found any pleasure in his embrace.

"The landlord's son was very handsome," she said dreamily. "His name was Raleigh Devereux and he smelled of soap and clean linen. He kissed me and told me that I was pretty, but it didn't mean anything to him; and after a while it didn't mean anything to me either. It was like a

71

dream, like one of Granda's tales that he never really expected me to believe. Michael was real, and he came from the same village, and so I married him."

"You need another man," Florrie repeated.

"When one comes, I'll know it," Tansy said slowly. "I'll know it deep inside myself, not at once maybe, but at some time when I'm not even thinking about him, then I'll know."

"God help all dreamers!" was Florrie's only reply, but she gave the younger girl a look in which contempt and compassion were oddly mingled. One day this odd little Irish girl would be badly hurt, unless she came down to earth and realised that men wanted only one thing and a woman was a fool to crave more.

Tansy, walking back to the shop a couple of nights later, was visited suddenly by the unnerving conviction that, if she didn't do something different, she would spend the rest of her life wearing a rut between Grub Street and Dryden Street. She knew the way so well that she could have walked it blindfold, and the thought brought not comfort but panic. For a moment she seemed to see herself grown old, still following the same route, shoulders a trifle bent, head poking forward towards the radiance cast by an occasional gas-jet.

If I go home now, Kate will be asleep, but the fire will still be burning and the kettle will be on the hob, she knew. I can warm my toes before the fire and brew a mug of tea and read a few pages of one of Mr. Schindler's books.

As she told herself that, her feet were turning in a different direction up Copperas Hill. The earlier rain had stopped, leaving a legacy of silver drops on the moonlit bushes in Raneleagh Gardens. It was still and quiet in this part of the city, so still that her own footsteps sounded like an echo.

Further up stood the four buildings she hated most in the whole of Liverpool. The gaunt and hopeless outlines of the workhouse, the lunatic asylum, the oakum sheds and the house of correction made a mockery of moon-silvered bushes. She had seen the convicts shuffling to their finger-tearing work, had heard the occasional yell of laughter from some face at a high, barred window, and failed to understand how people could take a trip to these places to stand and stare.

As for the workhouse, as long as she lived she would never forget seeing a group of children waiting to be admitted. They had stood quietly, with a patient, unchild-like look in their eyes, and she had wanted to scream and rage and take them all home with her. Then the big iron door had swung open and they had run inside. That seemed the most terrible thing of all, that they should run towards a life she could not even begin to imagine.

Tonight there were no yells, no clanking of chains nor measured tramp of feet. There was only the sound of music swelling high and sweet in the dark shadows. She thought the music was in her own head and stood still for a while, listening in pleasure. Then she became aware of the figure leaning against the wall just ahead. The tune ended with a flourish as she drew near and the man turned, lowering the fiddle and bow.

"I'm sorry but I haven't any money," she said awkwardly.

It embarrassed her that she hadn't even a copper to throw, but the fiddler spoke cheerfully.

"Surely, but it's no matter at all! I was playing for the pleasure of it."

"And I interrupted you!" She had a sense of guilt for having intruded.

"It was no interruption but an adding to the pleasure," he said gallantly, and fell into step with her as she walked on. "We always meet in darkness," he told her after a few minutes. "It's Tansy, isn't it? Tansy from Perimara?"

"And you are Donal, the fiddler. I thought you had travelled on; or were dead."

"I thought you were dead too," he said, and they both broke into laughter for the sheer delight of being alive.

"We live in Dryden Street above a milliner's shop," she said happily. "Kate helps out there and I serve down in the bar at the *Black Boy*. We get our food and keep, so it's not too bad."

"And I play where and when I can, and take whatever I can," he said.

"And your lodging? You do have a lodging?"

"In Lace Street. Aren't there a dozen or more of us crammed into a couple of rooms, and isn't the smell so bad that it makes your hair stand on end!"

But he was making it sound gay and comical, and they both knew it wasn't like that at all. It was hard, cold, homesickness much of the time, and only an occasional period of happiness to light up the wastelands in between.

"A man called Conrad Schindler owns the shop where we live," she said. "We have a parlour and a bedroom just for Kate and me, with two fireplaces and a carpet and a view from the window over all the houses. You can't see the dirt from up there, and it looks so pretty on a clear day."

"Faith, and aren't you the lucky one!" He gave her a friendly grin and a squeeze of the arm.

She was learning his face in patches as they moved in and out of gaslight and shadow. It was a lean face with long upper lip and high cheekbones. She could not glimpse the true colour of eyes or hair, but there was a brownness about him. Her Granda had been of the same shade, like a gnarled many-rooted tree. Donal was not as old as Granda had been, but something of what he possessed seemed now to be embodied in a stranger, so that he became no longer a stranger but somebody she remembered.

"Do the people like to hear you play?" she asked politely.

"When they've had a drink or two," he said, "they like to tap their feet to a jig or whistle to a reel. But late at night, when everything is quiet, I like to play for myself the tunes that I enjoy."

"It was a beautiful tune," she said.

"I made it myself, out of the melodies that crowd into my mind. One day I will find somebody who can write down music on paper and then I'll be a rich man."

"I can write words on paper," she regretted, "but not music."

"The writing of words is a grand thing," Donal said. "You ought to teach in a school instead of serving in a bar."

"I can't write as many words as a teacher would be needing," Tansy explained. "I wouldn't want to be a teacher anyway. Where's the sense of making somebody learn when there isn't a crying out in their hearts for it?"

They had reached the top of the hill and she paused, her head turning to look back over the dark city. Up here landmarks were obscured and a faint, yellow haze hung over the roofs, imparting a kind of enchantment to what, at dawn, would reveal itself as grimy and grey.

"When I have had all the music that is in me written down," Donal said, "I'll build a house up here with windows at each side of the door and settle myself there with a wife. We will be happy there and never quarrel."

"Your parents quarrelled?"

"Like cats and dogs," he said, "except I never heard a dog swearing at a cat, nor saw a cat beating a dog over the head with a saucepan. I used to set outside, listening until they fell asleep and I could get to my pallet in safety. When my mother died, it was the only time I ever saw my father cry. He only lived a few months after."

"And the fiddle?'"

"It belonged to an uncle of mine who used to come by two or three times a year. He drank like a fish and played like an angel, but he would never set his mind to any work. He left the fiddle with me one day, and I took it out into the fields and tried out a few notes."

"And so learned to play?"

"As if it were something I had forgotten already and began again to remember. When my uncle came back, he said the fiddle was mine now and sang for me."

"I don't remember my parents at all," she said, without much regret.

"Then you are fortunate. Parents are the greatest handicap a child can have," he told her gravely, and began to laugh again as if he spread ointment over a half-healed

76

wound.

"Will you come to supper one day?" she asked shyly. "I cannot cook yet at all, but Kate's dishes are good and filling."

"And would Kate cook something for me?"

"Indeed she would, and make you most welcome," Tansy said.

"And you would be there?"

"I get a night off now and then. I'll get one on Tuesday," she said.

"And I'll come to supper," he returned.

"To Dryden Street at eight o'clock. It's the little millinery shop at the right-hand side at the end."

"I'll be there," he was beginning, but Tansy, never one to spoil a good moment by prolonging it, was running back down the dark hill.

Edward, when asked if she might have the evening off, cocked an ugly eyebrow and informed her that for all the use she was she could take off three nights in a row.

Kate was less accommodating than she had imagined.

"You can't roam the streets and bring home anybody you happen to pick up," she complained.

"Donal isn't anybody," Tansy said indignantly.

"That's my point," Kate had on her sweetly patient face. "He's a street fiddler from Heaven knows where —"

"Connemara," Tansy put in.

"Living in Lace Street of all places, and not spending much time there if he's roaming about playing tunes in the middle of the night. And you want to bring him here. What will Mr. Schindler say?"

"He won't mind at all," Tansy said firmly. "Doesn't he

let us do as we please?"

In that she was right. Conrad Schindler, having taken the girls in, had left them free to do as they liked within the confines of the little shop. He was appalled at Tansy's attempts at decoration, though he was too kindly to tell her so, and he secretly deplored her habit of whistling loudly as she ran down the stairs each morning, for once woken he found it difficult to go to sleep again, but lay thinking of Rosa.

Kate's ways suited him better for she moved quietly and seldom spoke. She kept his rooms clean, and had sold two or three bonnets, and she was frugal with the housekeeping money he gave her. He had even found some rolls of material in the back of the store cupboard and Kate had patiently sewed neat brown dresses for herself and her sister.

Kate wore hers with a pink ribbon sash that gave her a demure, fairytale air. Tansy had cut up an old red tablerunner into leaves and sewn them around the neck and the hem. Some of the stitches had gone a trifle wobbly and the leaves were not all the same size, but if one didn't look too closely he supposed the effect was quite colourful.

"Mr. Schindler," Kate said now, "is a very patient old gentleman, and it must be hard for him to have his home turned upside down."

"He likes it," Tansy argued. "He has his house kept clean, and his clothes pressed, and his meals cooked, and someone to help in the shop, and all for the price of a week's housekeeping! He should be very grateful to us!"

It was the nearest they had ever come to quarrelling. Kate's cheeks were flushed and her eyes were over-bright.

Kate worked so hard and she was alone most of the day, Tansy thought with contrition. The only time she left the shop was when she went to market. And Kate was beautiful.

"Kate alanna, do you have anything left out of last week's money?" she asked.

"About five shillings. Why?"

"That would buy a nice bit of lamb and some apples for a pudding," she coaxed.

"Lamb on Tuesday!"

"Well, it's not a law that we can only have roast meat on Sunday," Tansy said reasonably. "And I'm sure he doesn't get a lot to eat. Please, Kate, just this once!"

"I wasn't planning on making a habit of it," Kate said with unaccustomed dryness, but Tansy had flung her arms about her in a fierce hug of gratitude.

Yet the evening, when it came, was not quite the success she had hoped. Kate had cooked the meat to perfection and baked tiny potatoes to set about it and the apple pudding was light and fluffy, but the formality of her greeting chilled even Donal's cheerful grin.

"Mr — er? My sister didn't mention your last name."

"O'Sullivan, ma'am. Not that folk ever call me by it. To them I'm just Donal the fiddler."

"And you have brought it with you! Did you expect to have to play for your supper?"

"No, ma'am, only for your pleasure," he returned, and Kate gave a nervous little smile as if she were not sure what her pleasure was and had no intention of telling him anyway.

Tansy had built up the fire herself, adding some pine

cones to sweeten it, and Donal huddled close to it, stretching thin hands to the blaze. He looked cold and shabby, his eyes deep-hollowed, and his coat too thin. Later when they sat at the table Kate relented a little and gave him the crispest portion of meat and an extra couple of potatoes, but though he ate everything, and praised the skill of the cook, conversation fell a little flat. It was a relief when he reached out for the fiddle and the strains of a traditional air stole through the room.

"Your sister doesn't like me," he said when, shortly after midnight, Tansy let him out into the street again.

"Kate is very shy," she defended.

"Kate thinks me a raggle-taggle you picked up out of the gutter and brought home to feed," he said, with so much truth that she crimsoned under cover of the darkness.

"But did you enjoy the meal?"

It seemed important to her that he should have relished the food.

"I enjoyed the company more."

"Kate is very beautiful," she agreed, but he took her hand.

"I was not speaking of Kate. I have been watching you all evening."

"And surely that was a great waste of time," she said lightly.

He was not to be deflected, however, but retained her fingers in a tight grasp and continued in a voice from which laughter had fled.

"I could make music out of your face, Tansy."

"And a poem out of my feet," she said flippantly.

"They would run ahead of the words," Donal said.

Holy Mother! Tansy thought in panic. The poor man is falling in love with me.

Under the panic, a small feeling of pleasure invaded her senses. It was, after all, something to be admired. If she were honest with herself it was the admiration that Michael O'Faolain had felt for her that had caused her to look at him with any interest in the beginning. She would have to remember that doglike devotion grew tedious after a while, and that Donal's odd resemblance to Granda which made him so comfortingly familiar would lack the charm of novelty.

"Anybody would think you'd been at the red biddy!" she rallied.

"Never a drop has passed my lips since last St. Patrick's Day."

His tone caught her mood and reflected it, but his eyes remained sombre. He was rangy rather than tall but she was so tiny that she had to bend her own head back slightly to meet his gaze. The gas-jet flared, illuminating the flat planes of his cheeks, the angle of his jaw.

"When I grow rich and build my house," he said swiftly as if he feared interruption, "I will ask you to be my wife and share it with me."

"You don't know me," she protested. "We haven't even met in daylight yet."

"I make up my mind on the instant," he told her. "I made it up when I spoke to you on the boat coming over, but when we landed, you and your sister were gone so quickly."

"And you didn't try to find me?"

"If you were still alive I knew we would meet again if

it was intended," he said simply.

"If I met a man and loved him," Tansy said, "I would follow him and find him if he were lost to me."

"Women are different," Donal said tranquilly, and he bent and kissed her mouth gently.

Perhaps it is I who am different from other women, Tansy thought. I never could sit still and let things happen to me. I always had to be up and doing, pushing events along.

She drew away, giving the warm, wide smile she reserved for those who interested her little.

"It's late," she said kindly. "You'd best go home."

"To Lace Street," he agreed wryly.

"And you wish that it were Connemara?"

"Connemara will never be as it was before the hunger began, and surely it's a grave mistake to be going back to a place where you were happy."

He kissed her again in a dreamy, lingering way, but she felt no answering passion, nothing save a vague regret that she had for him nothing more than friendliness and the kind of pity that is in itself a barrier to love.

"Did you enjoy your evening?" Edward enquired the next day as they dried tankards together.

"Very much," she began, then changed it to, "Not as much as I expected. It's strange, isn't it, how people you like don't always mix well when you bring them together?"

"It's not strange at all, and so your sense ought to tell you if you had any," Edward said crossly.

"His name is Donal," she said slowly, "and he talks of growing rich and of marrying me."

"And you? What do you talk of doing?" he asked.

"Of nothing," she said despondently. "Of nothing and nobody, as if I had died back in Ireland and only the shell of me lived here."

"That's because you're young and expect too much."

"Should I be like Florrie or like Annie?" she burst out. "I had a good husband, a good man, but I never loved him at all. Donal is like him, like my Granda too, but I cannot love him either."

"Then don't marry him."

"He's a fiddler drifting through the world and full of grand ideas, but they won't come to anything!" she cried angrily. "He wants a house with a window at each side of the door, high on the hill overlooking the city. He can at least put a name to his dream."

"Because it is a little one and your own dreams are larger than yourself. Dry that tankard properly and don't leave any smears on it or Malachy will have my hide."

Tansy made a face at his broad back and scrubbed furiously at the tankard. The bar was clean now, its sawdust fresh, its bottles gleaming, its tables scrubbed. By midnight it would be pungent with smoke and fumes, its floor scuffed and stained, its door banging noisily as customers tramped in and out. And she was trapped here with nothing more than her keep and a headful of cloudy, nameless dreams.

"When is the *Saranak* due in?" she asked abruptly.

"On Thursday. Why? Have you a fancy for a sailor lad?"

"I like to see the ship come in," she evaded. "I like to watch the sails against the sky, and the little waves slapping against the sides."

Jan Harrow had steady blue eyes and a long chin, and an

air of knowing who he was and what he wanted.

"When the weather is warmer," she told Edward, "I shall make Kate come up to Raneleagh Gardens and we'll eat our dinner there out of a basket. We'll wear our thin dresses and have cold meat and little red plums."

"And a stomach-ache in the afternoon," Edward said flatly. "Get on with your work and stop chattering!"

SIX

It was her seventeenth birthday, and on that day a girl was surely entitled to hope that something exciting would happen! Tansy put on the brown dress with the red leaves and whistled as she combed her hair. A free day lay ahead of her, for Malachy, to greet the spring, had decided to have the bar painted and the *Black Boy* was therefore closed until the task was finished. Under the comb her hair rippled red-gold, vibrant with life, and the colour was high in her cheeks.

If I were taller, she decided, and had a longer nose and a smaller mouth I would be as pretty as any of the ladies who ride in carriages.

Donal thought she was pretty already. He had told her so often since the night he had come to supper. She had not liked to ask him again and he was pursuing his courtship in a vague, amiable manner, sometimes seeing her three days in a row, and then vanishing for a fortnight.

Had she loved him it would have driven her crazy. As it was she seldom remembered him when he was absent and greeted his return with casual pleasure. He was on one of his periodic absences at the moment and she admitted to a sense of relief because the *Saranak* was in, and this time surely the stocky figure of Jan Harrow would stride down the gangplank.

She and Kate had coaxed a pair of shoes each out of the housekeeping money, but she had only her old shawl to cover her head. It was fast fraying into holes at the edges, but by folding it carefully she could disguise the worst of it.

"If you're going down into the market this morning can you get me a nice bit of fish?" Kate asked.

She was on her way downstairs to open the shop, her fair hair plaited in coils around her ears, a lacy apron hiding a darned patch on her skirt.

The market was near the docks. That meant a legitimate excuse for strolling along the quayside. She had watched the ships come in time after time, but on this particular day she would surely meet Jan Harrow again and it wouldn't do to appear to be waiting for him. Why he should turn up after five months' silence, or why she was anxious to meet him again, were questions she never bothered to ask herself.

It was one of those rare spring mornings when beauty casts a garland over the city. Sunshine ruffled the river, and a blue sky seemed to hold at bay the clouds of black smoke that billowed from the factories. Sprigs of green ventured from between the paving stones and many women, spurred into some kind of energy by the season, had whitened their doorsteps. The gulls were flying high, their calls thin and reedy above the cries and clangs of the dockyards. This part of Liverpool excited her because, though it was noisy and grimy, it had an optimism about it quite different from the grim purposefulness of the narrow alleys and slaughteryards.

Several of the regulars greeted her by name. Her frequent excursions to the dockside had insured her to some extent against insult. The witticisms patted in her direction were good-humoured and there were few to jostle her as she threaded her way between coils of rope and stacks of cargo.

The *Saranak* reared up against its backcloth of river and sky. She paused in the shadow of a high-laden wagon and watched the gangplank. If he walked down it now she could step casually out. Sentences rehearsed themselves in her head.

It's Jan Harrow, isn't it? How pleasant to meet you again! You probably won't remember me, but —?

"Surely it's the little Irish girl who was kind enough to keep me company at supper?"

The voice, frank and friendly, startled her so much that she whirled around, her hand clutching the rough wood of the wagon. He had come up from behind and for an instant shamed indignation flamed through her that he should have caught her gaping like a zany at the ship. If he had, however, he was too well-mannered to comment on the fact.

"I've often thought about you and hoped my path would lead me to Liverpool again."

"You're not with the *Saranak*?"

"I rejoined her a fortnight ago. For the past few months I've been at home, nursing a broken leg that refused to heal."

"You hurt hurself?" she said stupidly.

"I broke it, slipping on the deck like a greenhorn! My mother always said that if there was anything around to fall over I'd find it. Usually I heal up fast, but this time the bones wouldn't knit properly, and while I was laid up my sister decided to catch the measles so I went down with that too."

Broken limbs and measles — it scarcely made a romantic saga, and in her mind something of the glamour with which she had invested him was dispelled. His chin was definitely too long, his hair rougher than she recalled, and the nasal quality of his voice grated slightly on her ears.

"I hope you're better now," she said politely and wished desperately she could think of something clever and amusing to say. As it was there was nothing in her mind but a confused disappointment.

"Are you still settled here?" he asked.

About as settled as a bird on the branch of a winter tree, she thought; and answered brightly, "Kate and I have rooms now above a shop; a milliner's shop. She helps out there and I work at Malachy's tavern still. We are better off than many folk."

"And do you still go to Raneleagh Gardens after Mass?"

So he had remembered some part of their conversation. A little of her shyness fell away.

"Today is my seventeenth birthday. I promised Kate I'd buy some fish for supper tonight. I can buy enough for three if you'd like to come."

"If you'd do me the honour of coming to the theatre first," he began.

She interrupted him, gaspingly. "Holy Mother of God! but it's only grand ladies who go to the theatre. I've never been to one in all my life!"

"Then you must mark your birthday with your first

visit," he told her. "Shall I come with you to buy the fish, and then you can show me where you live, and I'll call back for you later."

For a moment excitement bubbled inside her. Then her mobile little face lengthened into gloom.

"I cannot come," she said. "Surely on my birthday it would be mean to leave Kate all by herself."

"Can't your sister go with us?" he enquired. "Or isn't the theatre to her taste?"

"She'd be wild to go, but I wasn't hinting," Tansy said swiftly.

It was on the tip of her tongue to protest that tickets for three were more expensive than tickets for two, but it wasn't ladylike to discuss money with a gentleman.

"Shall we buy the fish?" he asked, and took the little creel basket from her hand in a masterful manner which would have betrayed to a more experienced woman that he was still very young in many ways.

The fish had never looked so plump and shiny before; their eyes were scarcely glazed; their fins were crisply inviting. Conscious of his gaze she went importantly from stall to stall before choosing some firm white cod. Kate could do wonders with a butter sauce and some of the sweet, nutty potatoes that tasted so well baked in their jackets.

On the way home she added coffee and gingerbread and a crock of plum preserve to her small store. Her constraint had vanished, and she chattered freely as she led the way upward towards Dryden Street. They had an amicable wrangle over who was to carry the basket which ended with them swinging it between them.

It was, she decided, more fun to walk with a real young

man, even if his chin was too long and he'd been foolish enough to catch the measles, than to imagine a dream figure composed of her own romantic longings.

Kate was in the shop when they went in, and for a moment her fair hair and pale skin glowed against the dark interior. Then she came from behind the little counter to shake hands in her composed fashion as Tansy made hasty introductions.

"Kate, this is a friend of mine from America. You've heard me mention Jan Harrow, haven't you? And this is Kate, my sister."

"I'm afraid Tansy forgot to mention you," Kate said coolly, ignoring her sister's imploring look. "Are you a seafaring gentleman, sir?"

"He's an officer on board the *Saranak*," Tansy said.

"Your sister was kind enough to show me something of your city, ma'am," Jan said.

"I'm afraid that Tansy has a dreadful habit of wandering about and talking to strangers," Kate said with a tight, angry little smile.

"She surely made one stranger feel right at home, ma'am," Jan said placidly.

"Mr. Harrow has invited us both to the theatre tonight, Kate," Tansy put in swiftly. "It would be pleasant to go, wouldn't it?"

"Very pleasant." Kate's expression softened a little. "It's very kind of you, sir. We don't often get the opportunity of enjoying an evening out."

Now why, thought Tansy, can't I put things elegantly the way Kate does? Why can't I behave as if we were real ladies who often got invitations?

90

She stared at her sister with respect.

"Perhaps Tansy told you that it's her birthday today? After the theatre you might like to come back here for some supper?"

"That's truly kind, Miss Kate."

He had his hat in his hand and a smile on his face and Kate had lost her pinched defensive look. Tansy stood between them with the creel of fish and noticed that some of the leaves on her dress had come loose and hung ragged.

"If you ladies will excuse me," Jan was saying. "I'll call back for you around seven."

It was Kate who went with him to the door and came back, wrinkling her straight nose.

"Do take that fish into the kitchen, alanna," she said. "And tidy yourself up if you can. Mr. Harrow is a gentleman, I think, even if you did meet in an odd way. How *did* you meet him by the bye?"

"He'd lost his way and asked for directions," she said.

"And you never mentioned it to me? You're a queer one!"

"I forgot all about it," Tansy said.

"Well, go and tidy yourself — and get rid of that fish. Sure, it's stinking out the shop!"

Kate patted her smooth coils of gleaming hair and went back to the counter.

The day had dimmed a little, though she couldn't reason why. In the kitchen she gutted the fish and left them in cold water, and scrubbed the potatoes. Through the curtained alcove she could hear Kate talking to two customers. Her sister's sweet, indifferent tones chimed against hard, flat, local accents.

Since their arrival under Conrad Schindler's roof business had improved a little. At least five ladies a week went away with one of Rosa Schindler's creations perched upon her head. When the stock was diminished Kate intended to fashion new hats. Her thin fingers were nimble at the plaiting and weaving of ribbon and lace.

Mine, thought Tansy, looking ruefully at her discoloured palms, seem to be fit only for peeling potatoes and cleaning fish.

"Good morning, Miss Tansy. Is it not your birthday today?"

The inner door which led to Conrad Schindler's bedroom had opened, and he stood there, clad in a frayed and spotted smoking jacket and a pair of disreputable trousers.

"Yes, Mr. Schindler. I'm seventeen."

"Miss Kate told me of it."

He glanced about a shade nervously as he spoke. Kate had taken it upon herself to wash and mend his linen, and she would be far from pleased to see him arrayed in his oldest and most comfortable clothes. Tansy, however, appeared not to notice.

"Is it a morning off you're having?"

"One of my pupils is sick, and so I am at leisure." He came nearer, blinking a little behind his reading spectacles. "I have a little gift for you, Miss Tansy. It is a small gift, for I am a poor man, but for your birthday —"

He trailed off, putting a small package in her hands.

"I wrote the stories down when Rebecca was no more than five years old," he said shyly. "I used to tell her little tales, you understand, so that she would be a good child

92

and go quickly to sleep. Rosa thought that such tales might be gathered together and sold, but my English then was not so fluent and nobody would buy. But I made the book over many years, and then Rebecca died, and I laid it away."

"I shall read them all," she said truthfully. "I never had a book of my own before!"

To be able to read was a grand thing, but to have actually written a book —

Misty with gratitude, she said happily. "This is a fine day! You give me a book of my very own, and a young gentleman is taking Kate and me to the theatre this evening."

"The theatre?" He looked at her vaguely. "Rosa was very fond of the play. We used to go two or three times a year. She would put up her hair and wear a very striking dress — plum coloured it was, with little flounces of cream lace. Other gentlemen used to admire her."

Rosa had put on too much weight to fit comfortably into the dress during the latter years, but he could see her in it still, with her black hair swept up above her ears.

Still vague, but conscious that Tansy's outfit looked a trifle crumpled, he enquired, "And what will you be wearing, Miss Tansy? Something gay to greet the spring?"

"I never thought about it!"

She looked at him in astonished dismay, having completely neglected to remember that neither she nor Kate owned the sort of dress in which a lady would visit the theatre. The green dress she wore for work was stained and patched and her brown one, despite its gay, ragged leaves, was an everyday gown and not intended for evening wear.

"There are some dresses that Rosa wore," he said hesitantly. "But she fell ill, you see, and they were laid away, hardly used. If you would like to take a look —?"

He nodded towards a corner cupboard in the inner room. Kate had cleaned the room several times and regularly rearranged the books and ornaments that littered it. Equally regularly they became disarranged again and a fine film of dust spread itself over the carpet. The cupboard, however, was neatly arranged and smelled of lavender as if Rosa had put her gowns away herself in the hope of wearing them again.

"They're a bit roomy for me," Tansy said doubtfully, lifting out a blue one and matching it against her small frame.

"Ja! my Rosa was a big, fine woman!" Conrad Schindler said proudly.

"But if Kate could take a couple of them in at the waist and turn up the hems — you do mean that my sister is to wear one too?"

"But of course. For too long have they hung there. It is better they should be seen. I will leave you to make your choice."

He shuffled out, as if it pained him to watch a young, healthy girl fingering his dead wife's possessions.

Rosa Schindler had evidently favoured vivid colours and heavy materials to suit her black hair and sallow skin and full-bosomed majesty of figure. Tansy, loving bright colours too, plunged her hands into dark red and sapphire and the richness of maroon. For herself she craved the dark red, but Kate needed a gentler colour. There was a silvery grey faintly striped with red and decorated with tiny ruffles of lace.

"Mr. Schindler says that we may choose a dress each and a bonnet each from stock to wear tonight. Isn't it generous of him?" Kate remarked as she came through with her silent step.

"It was lovely of him!" Tansy agreed with enthusiasm.

There was a filmy lace scarf against which Kate's white skin would glow creamily.

"I hoped that you would have asked him to share our little supper after the theatre," Kate said.

"Asked him — I never thought of it! Oh, Kate, how awful of me!"

Tansy swung round, her cheeks flushing as red as the gown in her arms.

"Fortunately *I* did." Kate gave her a sweet, amused glance. "I do wish you could learn to be a trifle more considerate. A lady is judged by such things."

"Then I suppose that I'll never be a lady," Tansy said ruefully.

"But we can both look like ladies in these," Kate murmured, the sting of her sweetness withdrawn. "I'll close the shop early and get down to the altering. For the love of all the saints, Tansy, go and scrub your hands. Surely the fish smell will be clinging to these pretty things!"

The rest of the day passed in a whirl of fittings and alterations. Tansy was only too thankful that Kate could sew quickly and skilfully, for left to herself she would never have been able to make a start on the elaborate pleating and tucking required before even the narrowest dress moulded itself to her small bust and waist.

95

They were ready before time, Kate elegant in the silvery grey with a tiny bonnet of chip straw on her smoothly coiled hair, Tansy hopping impatiently from window to chair and back again until her cheeks were as scarlet as her dress. It had been impossible to find a bonnet that didn't clash with the gown, but Kate had tied her hair back with loops of white ribbon. Already several strands of hair had escaped from their silken fetters and were tumbling down her neck.

"The meal is ready to be cooked and the table laid," Kate said with satisfaction. "Do close the bedroom door. You'd not be wanting to show the gentlemen where we sleep."

Tansy, who had imagined herself revealing the grand little bed she had all to herself, closed the door meekly. From the street below came the rumbling of wheels and the jangling of harness.

She was at the window in a flash, waving her hand as she exclaimed, "He's come for us in a coach! Kate, there's a real coach down there for us to ride in!"

"It's a hired brougham. No need to act as if you'd never seen one before," Kate said, adjusting her bonnet slightly in the glass.

"Well, I've never ridden in one!"

Picking up the full red skirts that were still, despite Kate's efforts, a trifle too long, Tansy flew down the narrow stairs.

Confronting the fair, stocky young gentleman, however, she was assailed by a shyness that muted her tongue and dyed her face a more hectic red. He seemed afflicted by the same shyness for he twisted his hat nervously in his hands and looked positively relieved as Kate came serenely to greet him.

"You are a little before time, but none the less welcome," she said smilingly.

Her words, Tansy thought, were so exactly those that a lady would use and her outstretched hand was untrembling. She was even beginning to lose her Irish brogue a trifle, and the unconcern with which she stepped up into the brougham would have convinced the most suspicious observer that she was used to riding in a carriage every day of her life.

Tansy, bouncing on the soft leather of the seat, held on to the strap that hung by the window and peered out in silent excitement at the streets. She had walked them night and morning, but to ride through them, to look at them through glass, invested them with an excitement rendered more potent by a soft twilight that purpled the shadows and cast a patina of gold over the cobblestones.

Kate and Jan Harrow were talking like old friends. It was a long time since Kate had looked so pretty and surely she had never sounded so lively. When her pretty laugh rang out Tansy felt as content as if she had caused the amusement herself.

The *Theatre Royal* was all carved pillars, and a sweeping staircase that for a moment reminded Tansy of the great house at Devereux Place. But there were paintings of laides and gentlemen in wigs and costumes on the walls and the ceilings were decorated with golden cherubs and sea-horses, and a pair of helmeted ladies only partly con-cealing their ample charms behind wisps of painted drapery.

97

They had what Kate whispered was "a box". It was set, rather disappointingly, at the side of the stage and quite a number of ropes and pulleys could be glimpsed behind the red plush curtain with its golden fringe.

"Mother of God, but my dress is the same colour as the curtains!" Tansy exclaimed.

There were stifled giggles from a group of young ladies directly below where they sat. Kate leaned back, paling a little as if she had received an insult, but Tansy, grinning ruefully at her own bad breeding, leaned over to get a better view of the audience as the people streamed in. They were, she decided, a mixed bunch; the better-dressed and more quietly behaved occupying the middle seats, while a more colourful and vociferous mob filled up the pit and the high galleries.

And then she forgot the people, and the chattering, and the strains of music that set her feet tapping and waves of excitement shivering up her back. She clasped her hands tightly in her lap and opened her eyes wide as the gaslight dimmed.

Slowly the heavy curtain rose, hesitated midway and rose again as the music swelled to a crescendo.

She had forgotten the young man who sat between Kate and herself. She had forgotten her new red dress and the hair tumbling from its white ribbon. The world was become a framed picture, where men and women, with paint thick on their faces, and legs encased in tight breeches, or hidden under the swaying petals of widespread skirts, danced and sang, laughed and cried in voices that rang through the great building.

She laughed with them, sobbed when the heroine's aged

98

father died, held her breath when the moustachioed villain strode on, hissed with everybody else when his perfidy was unmasked, and felt a bitter-sweet fluttering of the senses when hero and heroine clasped hands against the painted backdrop of a vessel with sails unfurled under a silver moon.

She was sitting in the cramped, red-curtained little box, and the palms of her hands were red with clapping. Kate was leaning forward slightly, her lips parted, her grey eyes shining. Jan Harrow had turned his head towards her. A box of chocolates lay open on the ledge. Tansy remembered vaguely that there had been an interval.

They were standing now as the voices of the audience blended into a ragged Anthem. The girls in the seats below were shrugging themselves into capes and tiny jackets with big collars.

Tansy was unreasonably surprised when they came out into the street to see that it was quite dark. There was a thrill for her in the press of people and the crying of the baked potato-sellers with their glowing carts.

"I told the cab man to come back after the performance," Jan was saying.

The music had followed them into the street. She stood, feet tapping on the kerb, and looked around, her bright amber gaze piercing the darkling crowd. Then she saw the music was made by one shabby man who filled the narrow street with melody.

"Donal?"

She had spoken his name in glad surprise at meeting a friend again, but her voice wasn't heard above the crowd. Yet something must have penetrated the music that filled his mind, because he stopped playing for an instant and looked straight at her.

"Miss Tansy, shall we hurry before somebody else takes our cab?"

Jan Harrow's hand, square and blunt fingered, rested tentatively on her scarlet sleeve. The music began again and dragged into a discord as she turned away.

"What a lovely play it was!" Kate was saying happily.

"A real grand one!" Tansy agreed, and forgot the fiddle music as the shelter of the brougham enfolded her.

SEVEN

"The *Saranak* is due this evening. I suppose that means you'll be wanting the night off," Edward said sourly.

"I'll come in, if you think we're going to be busy," Tansy offered.

"We're busy every night, and it doesn't make a particle of difference whether you're here or not!"

Edward flapped a cloth pettishly, his shoulder heavy with sulking.

"I think I'll come in," Tansy said casually. "Kate can go down to meet the ship if she likes."

"And spend the evening with the worthy sailor-boy? Doesn't he ever get tired of being shared?"

"It's not a bit like that!" she flamed, "We're friends. The three of us are friends!"

"A neat little triangle," he smirked. "What will happen when sailor-boy fixes his fancy on one of you? What will the other do then, I wonder?"

"You wonder about other people's business too much," she said shortly.

"Because I've none of my own. But I can make good guesses from time to time." He put his massive head on one side and regarded her ironically. "It's my guess that you keep pushing Kate at sailor-boy because you're not quite certain. And it's my guess that you won't make up your mind because if you did fall in love with him there'd be sister Kate all by herself."

"Jan likes us both equally," she defended. "And it's for the gentleman to choose the lady."

"Tell that to the fairies!"

He flapped the cloth at her again and minced clumsily through the door to speak to Florrie.

Tansy stared after him in exasperation. Edward was ugly, unnatural, foul-tempered and too frequently right. She was always promising herself that one day she would walk out of the *Black Boy* and never go back. Then she would remind herself that, even if she received no wages, the job provided her with two good meals a day.

But more than that held her to it, though she was only half-aware of the reasons herself. It was bound up with the colour and vigour of life in the bar compared to the genteel dimness of the little hat-shop, to the rough teasing of Edward and Florrie that had about it a warmth that was absent in Kate's gentle chiding.

If she could only fall whole-heartedly in love with Jan everything would be so much simpler; but though she liked him immensely the only time she felt romantic about him was when he was away.

"I wish I didn't always want what I can't have," she said dismally to her reflection in the glass behind the bar.

Her face scowled back at her, short-nosed, wide-mouthed, with eyes that slanted under winged brows. Her skin looked sallow and there was a hard little frown between her eyes.

In ten years' time she would look haggard with all her soft youth dried into disappointment. In twenty years' time, when she had put on a little weight and the red-gold of her hair was marred with grey, she would begin to look like Florrie. In thirty years —!

"I'm going out for a bit of a walk," she called in the direction of the kitchen passage and ran through the front door without waiting for a reply.

It was warm for September with only the faintest chill in the air to warn of the approaching winter. Her feet turned automatically towards the docks where the constant bustle and movement compensated for the smell of tar and rope and rotting fish, and the beauty of the great ships overshadowed the darkness of the warehouses and coal-yards.

The *Saranak* was already in, which meant she had had favourable winds and a strong tide. Tansy had sometimes pictured herself standing on the heaving deck with spray lashing her face and the salt breeze whipping her hair about her shoulders. Today the breeze was gentle, and dappled the high decks. Tansy remembered how she had stood, watching the gangplank, waiting for the figure of her imaginings to descend. And, after all, he had turned into a plain, pleasant young man whose parents kept a store in Boston and who paid equal court to her sister and herself. But if she really thought hard about it —!

Mother of God, but I can *make* myself fall in love with him! she told herself. I can make him want to marry me too, if I put my mind to it. The poor young man only wants a push in the right direction.

She would run home and put on the red dress and

borrow the straw bonnet out of the shop window. The dress had been so seldom worn that there were only a couple of grease marks on it, and the brim of the bonnet would shade her face in an interesting and mysterious way.

Tansy had already turned when she caught sight of them walking along the quayside. Their backs were towards her, but the sunlight gleamed on the coils of hair that tilted back Kate's small head. She had laid her hand on Jan's arm and her tinkling laughter floated back to where Tansy stood, unnoticed by either of them.

I would like, Tansy thought, to jump on a boat and go straight home to Perimara.

There would be people still in the village who had known her when she was a little girl, and scolded her for being untidy and mischievous. The scarred land would be healed now and the flowers thick in the long grass of Devereux Park. There was nothing to keep her in the dirty, noisy city whose pavements hurt her feet and the accents of whose citizens offended her ears. There might even be a boy for her to marry, and if there wasn't, then glory be to God! but she could keep house for Father MacNabb!

She turned towards Victoria Dock, not casting one backward glance at the high, proud *Saranak*. The home-sickness she had held at bay for more than a year washed over her, wrenching her heart.

"Will you be looking where you're going now, or do you hope to be walking straight into the sea?" Donal asked, seizing her firmly by the shoulders.

"Let me alone! I'm going home!" she said crossly after her first start of recognition.

"And doesn't Dryden Street lie in the other direction

entirely?"

"To Ireland, you fool! I'm going home to Perimara."

"And what will you be using for passage money?" he enquired. "Or were you thinking of swimming?"

"I came over as ballast and I can go back the same way. If not —" She hesitated, putting pleading into her voice and eyes. "If not, you'll lend me the passage money, won't you?"

"If you can give me a good reason, darling, for wanting to run away."

"I'm not wanting to run away," she glared. "Surely it's a natural thing to be craving home!"

"And the people of home." He nodded, his thin face sombre. "Who will be waiting at home to welcome you back?"

"Why there's —"

She stopped, staring back at him while her mind shaped and discarded familiar names. Not Bridie, the eldest sister who had reared her from babyhood. Bridie had turned her face to the wall, and drifted into death.

Not her brothers, Seamus and Patrick. Seamus had taken his wife and the rent money and run away; and Pat was dead.

Not Granda, who had been the anchor of her childhood. He was dead too. And not Michael, her husband, whose bones rotted now somewhere in the Dublin gaol.

"There isn't anybody," she said at last, and began to cry forlornly. "There isn't anybody at all!"

"Then there's no sense in going back," Donal said, and he put his arms round her, and held her tightly as if she were the only thing in the world that he valued.

"What are you doing down here anyway?" she demanded, drawing away and rubbing her eyes with the corner of her shawl. "And you've not got your fiddle with you!"

"God help me, but I left the darling thing at home!" He released his grip slightly and smiled at her.

"Then what are you doing here?"

"Watching the pretty boats sail in and sail out again," he said flippantly, and then, growing serious as if he had decided she was old enough to bear the truth, he said, "Did you not hear the news then? Surely the newsboys have been crying it all over town all day!"

"Crying what? I've been in the bar all day."

"Darling, do you go round with your ears stopped up and the eyes of your heart shut tight? The crops in Ireland have failed again."

"The potato crop? Oh, *no*! Donal, no! The same thing couldn't happen again!"

Her cry of dismay was for the long months of misery and the slow dying that lay like a stone on her memory.

"Alanna, but it has. The sweet plants have blackened again and soon every boat will be packed with those who flee the famine. Now isn't it a bad time for you to be thinking of going home!"

"Then what am I to do?" She looked at him so hopefully that his own vision blurred a little.

"Come to my rooms in Lace Street," he invited. "You've not been entertained with a dish of tea and a tune yet, have you?"

He was too good-hearted to remind her, but she saw, in his eyes, the picture of herself in the red gown stepping out of the theatre while he stood shabby on the corner playing his song to an uncaring world.

"I'd like to come," she said, and was a little ashamed of the pleasure that leapt into his face as he tucked her hand into his arm.

The room was worse than she had expected. It was too small and too dark and there was not even the pretence of cleanliness. The criticism that he might have made some effort to make it habitable trembled on her lips.

"Sit yourself comfortably while I make the tea," Donal said cheerfully.

He disappeared down an evil-smelling passage where he could be heard chattering dishes and whistling.

The wallpaper was tattered, the small grate choked with ashes, the mattress rumpled. She sat down on it cautiously, there being no chair, and wondered uneasily if she were growing proud. There had been a time when she would not have noticed dirt at all, but over the past year she had imperceptibly changed. Kate kept their own rooms over the shop as neat as a new pin, and Edward had a feminine horror of dirt.

"There's your tea," Donal announced, returning with two steaming mugs. "Hot and black with a dash of poteen in it to cheer you up."

"Who lives in this place?" She took the mug of tea and looked about her.

"A couple of tinkers drift in and out, when they feel like it, and there's a fellow from Donegal way who's waiting for his wife to join him, if the poor soul is still alive. She stayed behind to nurse her old mother through her last days, but he's had no word from her since though he goes down to meet every boat."

"Kate and I were lucky," she said sombrely. "They're packed twenty to a room in William Henry Street and half the girls are walking the streets."

She was lucky, she reflected, not to be walking them herself. Give Malachy half a chance and he'd have her on Annie's beat. Sometimes it crossed her mind that if Edward didn't protect her so carefully from the attentions of the customers she might have found herself long since parading in tattered finery down New Scotland Road.

"And you and Kate have two rooms for the two of you," he marvelled. "And after she's gone —"

"Gone? Where would Kate go?" she asked sharply.

"The young gentleman she was with at the theatre. And I've caught glimpses of them since in Raneleagh Gardens. Isn't he Kate's fancy?"

"Jan is a friend to both of us," Tansy said, setting down the half-drained mug carefully on the soiled floor. "He's American. An officer in the Navy."

"Very solid and steady from the looks of him," he commented, dropping to the mattress beside her and stretching out his legs.

"He's a gentleman," she told him frostily.

"And on the lookout for a sweet little wife to take home to his family? Or has he got a wife already?"

"No he has not!" she said, nettled.

"Then he'll be looking for one, and Kate is neat and pretty. What about a dowry?"

"Dowry?" She blinked at him stupidly.

"He's a gentleman. Gentlemen expect a bit of a dowry to come along with the bride."

"Jan knows that Kate and I have no money at all."

Kate Alanna

"And he hasn't married her yet which means he's still thinking about it. Now I'm not a gentleman, and I don't have that problem."

"No, Donal. No."

She put out a hand to ward him off, but his arms were about her again and his breath was hot on her neck.

"I've told you before that one day I'd build a fine house at the top of the hill," he was saying. "I said then that I'd ask you to live in it with me. But I don't want to wait, Tansy. I want to marry you now."

"It seems a pretty drastic way of getting a better place to live," she said feebly.

"Mother of God! but I don't care a damn where we live! It's you I want, the warmth and the laughter of you and the way your eyes dance when you're amused and flash when you're out of temper! I know I'm not good enough for you, alanna. I know that. I've kept away from you for months, telling myself that it wasn't any use, but when I saw you again today I knew I had to ask you."

"I'm not ready. I haven't thought about it," she stammered.

"For the love of all the saints what is there to think about?" he demanded. "If Kate weds her American she'll be off to the States anyway, and if she doesn't, can't you find a corner for me somewhere without bursting the walls? My fiddle doesn't take up much room."

"Couldn't you get a job?" she asked.

"Haven't I got one already?" he retorted. "Don't I play my fingers to the raw bones squeezing money out of the stony-hearted English? Can I help it if nobody is listening to good music any longer? You're arguing for the sake of it, darling. You don't want to be arguing with me now, do you?"

Tansy shook her head. At that moment she didn't know what she wanted. Part of her was repelled by the room and the sour whisky smell on his breath; part of her craved the comfort of his arms, and the warmth of his body pressed close against her own.

"It's not a time for arguing, now is it?" he whispered.

She would have shaken her head but his hands had crept up to her hair and his mouth sought her own. For an instant, something bright and hot gleamed faintly and struggled for release. Then, just as swiftly, it had died and she was empty again — quiet and empty.

He was pushing her dress down over her shoulders and the cold air struck her breasts. She had not realised before how chilly it was in the ugly little room. Better to close her eyes and remember only that Donal was kind and had dreamed a dream of her.

"It isn't any use at all, is it?" said his voice.

His hands had dropped to his sides again and his mouth had a hurt, unhappy grin upon it.

"I'm sorry," she said dully. "I'm so sorry, Donal. I like you so much —"

"But it isn't enough?"

"Perhaps there's something wrong with me," Tansy said miserably. "Perhaps I'm lacking something.

"It's the room," Donal said. "You're not a girl to keep in a room like this. Surely I should have waited until I'd built the grand house on the hill."

"Surely that would be better," she agreed, and pulled up her gown, glad of the excuse to look away.

"Shall I be playing you something before you leave?" he asked.

"That would be fine," she said politely.

If he would only take her in his arms again, force her into some pretence of loving, make her forget the cold and the dirt! But he had moved away, tucking the fiddle under his chin, fitting his fingers to the bow.

A gay tune mocked their mutual unhappiness. He should, she thought, have played a dirge. The music was tactless and tasteless, and it made her want to weep.

"I ought to be going back to work," she said at last.

"I'll walk with you," he said, but she shook her head, rising and wrapping her shawl about her as if to repel any further invasion of her person.

"It's late. I'd best run," she said.

"I'll see you again?"

He had stopped playing and the silence was worse than the tune.

"Of course you will," she said warmly, hating herself. "You must come to supper again."

"So that sister Kate can look down her nose at me?" He gave her a bitter little smile. "I'll wait until she's married her gentleman from America, and by then I shall have begun to build the house."

"The house on the hill, yes."

She nodded and gave him a quick, kind smile.

"And I'll not be giving up," he said staunchly. "There'll be a day when you'll tell me you love me. I know it in my bones, darling."

"And no doubt but you're right," she said, and let herself out quickly into the unlovely street.

The gay melody pursued her as she hurried away and then was lost in the hooting of the ships' sirens as the first hint of September fog spread itself over the river.

"You took a long walk," Edward said when she let herself into the bar.

"The potatoes have failed again," she said briefly. "There'll be more of us pouring into the city before the month is out."

"And the city council screaming the place is full already, and the rates going up to support a crowd of illiterates who won't lift a finger to take care of themselves."

Florrie was leaning, arms folded, against the corner of the bar. She seldom bothered to come into the saloon but now her blackcurrant eyes surveyed Tansy with malicious amusement.

"The English government should have done something to make certain the same thing didn't happen again," Tansy retorted. "The landlords should go back and work their own land and let us keep the profits to improve ourselves instead of filling the pockets of greedy agents."

"Get away with you!" Florrie teased. "No Irishman ever did a decent day's work in his life."

"That isn't so!" Tansy flared. "An Irishman will work as hard as the next man if he sees any sense in what he's given to do. The English set our men to building roads — only the roads didn't even lead anywhere, and men lay down and died of starvation, although the Dublin granaries were packed to bursting with corn and wheat."

"You should give the girl a box and make her go to St. George's Hall to make a political speech," Florrie told Edward.

"Not until she's finished her work here," Edward said tranquilly. "And if you're looking for Maggie she sneaked in about half an hour ago up the back stairs."

"I'll have her hide!"

Effectively diverted, Florrie tugged her improbably red hair into place and heaved her bulk through the inner door.

"The *Saranak* is in already," Tansy said casually.

"Is that where you've been?"

"I met Donal," she evaded. "He wants to marry me, you know."

"Which would be the silliest thing you could do," Edward told her.

"I'll have to marry somebody, I suppose," she said thoughtfully.

"You've time enough before you walk down the aisle again," Edward said.

"And Donal would take me without a dowry."

"If he were a rich man there'd be some sense in his generosity. Couple over in the snug want some whisky. Is it or isn't it your job to serve them?"

She served them and came back to the bar, returning to the subject like a dog worrying a bone.

"Kate doesn't have a dowry either. Do you think Jan Harrow would marry her without one?"

"He's a shopkeeper's son, isn't he? Of Dutch descent?" At her nod he said decisively: "Well, there you are then! He's too cautious to make a move until he's worked out all the possibilities. But I thought Jan Harrow was your young man."

"He's friendly with both of us," she said, echoing her words to Donal.

113

"But if one of you had a dowry, it might help to make him friendlier in one direction?"

"You make him sound —"

"Like a sensible young man? The fiddler isn't sensible, I take it. Which one do you prefer?"

"It isn't a question of choice!" she said crossly.

From the other side of the saloon a man called impatiently; "Are you serving drinks tonight or getting into corners with Edward?"

"I'm coming. I'm coming."

She set tankards in a row and splashed red biddy into them with a carelessness that earned her a frown and a sharp poke in the ribs from Edward.

When she came out of the *Black Boy* at midnight, Jan was waiting for her. He seldom appeared at her place of work, but the fog had grown thicker and she was glad of his company.

"Kate was worried about you," he said. "The streets aren't safe for young ladies these days."

"I never have any trouble — but then I'm not a young lady," she joked.

"It worries me too having you work in a place like that," he said. "You and Kate have done so well, getting yourselves out of Ireland and over here. But you can't work in a bar for the rest of your life."

"It's the best I can find for the moment," she said.

"Well, at least Kate is out of it. I just couldn't have borne to think of that fragile girl serving liquor to that riff-raff."

"They're not so bad," she said curtly. "A lot of them are decent folk, as decent as you'd find aboard ship."

"I'm not denying it! And I'm not criticising you. Lord knows you've done the best you can and it's not been easy, but you and Kate ought to be thinking about the future."

"That's our concern," she frowned and softened it with, "Anyway you've your own future to consider."

"And I don't mind telling you that I'm plumb disenchanted with seafaring."

"Then what will you do?"

"Go home and work in the store, I guess. Pick me a pretty little wife."

His fingers tightened on her arm and the fog muffled his features.

"You can't think how much it's meant to me, having you and Kate as friends. I wrote and told my folks all about you and they were truly grateful for the way you've made me feel at home."

"It was our pleasure," she said in a small voice.

"Well, there'll be things to discuss," he said vaguely. "Lots to talk over before I hand in my ticket."

She sensed obscurely that she had been granted a reprieve but she didn't know from what. The choice, after all, wasn't hers to make.

EIGHT

"So that's the way of it, you see," Edward said.

"But it's not possible!" Tansy stared at him in disbelief. "People don't just up and die unless they're sick. You're not sick! I never saw a fitter man."

"If you had in your bowels the burning that I have in mine you'd not speak so lightly of it," Edward said grimly. "And I'm not asking for sympathy, so you may take that moist look out of your eye. I'm past fifty and I've had a good run for my money, so there's no reason to jump into mourning! It's not as if I've a family to bother my head about. When the time comes I'll up and off, quiet as a mouse, and the regulars can have a drink in my memory. No, it's you I've been thinking about."

"Me?"

"Now don't get the notion into your head that I'm fond of you," Edward said hastily. "I've seen prettier girls with better dispositions come and go here in my time, and most of them ended up like Annie walking some godforsaken beat. But you've got something they hadn't. I can't put a name to it rightly, but it's a kind of bounce in your nature that puts you right back on top two minutes after you've

116

been knocked down. That's why I let you go on helping me here, for the Lord knows you're more trouble than you're worth. Malachy and Florrie were for throwing you out when you wouldn't walk the beat, but I talked them out of it."

"That was nice of you," she said, grateful and confused.

"The point is," Edward said, "what's to become of you when I've gone. Eh, girl?"

"I'll go on working in the bar, I suppose."

"As to that, you must please yourself. If the new manager is willing to put up with you, then that's his bad luck. But Malachy won't pay for your work. He and Florrie are tighter than two tits when it comes to money."

"So?"

Tansy tried to make her voice cool and indifferent, but inside another voice questioned miserably.

Why does Edward blather on about things that don't matter when he's just told me that he's going to die? He's been a better friend to me than I ever realised or he'd ever admit, and he goes on and on about things that don't matter.

"I'm not a rich man," Edward said, "but I've saved up a bit. Most of it's for Annie and the girls, if Florrie lets them get a smell of it; but I want you to have your share now. Call it a dowry if you like."

"But I can't!"

Dismayed, she stared at the leather bag he was thrusting into her hands. It was so heavy that her wrists ached as they took the strain.

"You hide it somewhere in that home from home where I've never been invited," he said grumpily.

"There must be a thousand pounds here!" she gasped.

"Two hundred, in solid coin, and I've bitten the edge of every one of them! Put it away and use it as a dowry when you've made up your mind which one you want to marry. And if you say a single word more I'll take the lot back and give it all to Florrie!"

"It's very good of you," she said timidly, and might have kissed him but he backed away scowling, so she contented herself with a quick pat on his massive arm.

"You can use up your energy on those tables," he said. "They're a disgrace with all those marks on them. You'd better give them an extra polish to keep you out of mischief. And tie that bag to your petticoat. No sense in me saving up for years so that somebody can come along and hit you over the head and grab the lot!"

It was, in Tansy's eyes, a small fortune. Two hundred pounds would buy her immediate release from the necessity of having to work at the *Black Boy*, but even as the gladness of the thought lifted her spirits she knew it would be impossible to leave yet. Edward would never admit it, but he needed her help. His last words before she went home that night were a warning.

"Don't go babbling my private affairs all over Liverpool. If Malachy got wind of what's afoot he'd put a younger man in before either of us could turn round!"

Tansy had promised, mentally exempting Kate from the rest of Liverpool.

"It means a hundred pounds each," she told her sister. "It could serve as dowry if — if either of us ever wished to wed."

"It's a great deal of money," Kate trickled the coins

118

through her slim fingers. "I suppose Edward has been cheating on the bar profits for years."

"I never thought about it!"

"Ah, well, it's ours now and not our business to enquire. I'll ask Mr. Schindler to lock it in his safe until the time comes for us to be needing it. No sense in frittering it away."

Kate was scooping the money into the bag, drawing the leather cord tight.

"You could stop working in that dreadful place now," she pointed out.

"I thought of that, but if Edward is truly so ill, it wouldn't be fair to walk out," Tansy excused.

"And you enjoy working there, don't you?" Kate regarded her sadly and gravely. "You always did enjoy running wild, even when we were children."

Standing in a hot, smoky room, carrying heavy trays, scalding her fingers in near-boiling water were not activities that Tansy would have classed as running wild, but she let the subject drop.

The new year of eighteen forty-nine brought with it the inevitable rain and an increasing number of immigrants, fleeing from the hunger. Sometimes Tansy went down to the Victoria dock and watched the ferry boats disgorge their human cargo. They streamed down the gangplank in a muddle of shawls and caps and string-tied packages and feeble, whining children. Some had relatives to meet them, but many of them seemed to be alone and these invariably paused on the stone wharf looking with a kind of dull horror at the grimy warehouses that shut out the grimier sky.

"Mother of God!" she heard one woman say. "Are there no green fields in this England!"

She had wanted to tell her that on the outskirts of the city were parks and gardens where ladies in pretty dresses strolled on fine days, but few had the strength or will to climb so far. It was easier to squeeze oneself into an overcrowded, unventilated basement and to spend one's coppers on the gin or red biddy that brought a temporary oblivion. It was quite usual these days to see men and women staggering drunkenly at midday and fallen into the gutters by teatime. It seemed to Tansy that all these people had but one face, vacant, sly and despairing and one whining voice that begged for work and food in the slurred accents of a hopeless nation.

"It's foolish to upset yourself so," Kate scolded when Tansy came home heavy-eyed. "There isn't a thing in the world you can do for any of them, except pray."

Kate prayed regularly, both in church and late at night at the side of her bed. Her voice was no more than a sweet murmur, but she rose with a peaceful look on her face as if she had been receiving personal reassurances from the Almighty. Tansy envied her, for her own prayers had become disjointed and useless, and her faith comfortless.

"You care too much," Conrad Schindler told her. "You care too much about people, Miss. Tansy. It is wiser to grow a little hard."

Edward put it more bluntly.

"You feel guilty, girl, because you have a decent roof over your head and regular vittles, so you go down to the docks and weep crocodile tears for people you can't help and wouldn't even want to know if the chance jumped up

120

and hit you on the cheek! Half these folk make a religion out of feeling sorry for themselves, but they'll not raise a finger to lift themselves out of the mire."

She supposed there was some sense in what he said, but she continued to go down to the quay, to watch the over-laden boats draw slowly in, to hear echoed in a dozen brogues the sentence that summed up the feelings of those who landed.

"Mother of God, there are no green fields in this England!"

She had gone down one blustery March day, ostensibly to buy some fish, for Kate hated the market stench and feared the obscenities of the fishwives with their keen knives and scale-thick hands. Inevitably she had turned towards the harbour, drawn there by the salt-wind blowing up the estuary, and by a half-formed reluctance to go back to the dim little shop.

At one end of the wharf a knot of men squatted, rolling dice idly, their caps low on their foreheads. Further on a ring of children joined hands around a dead and bloated cat as if they were taking part in some pagan right. A couple of whores, leaning against the low wall in small hope of a client, greeted her loudly by name. In the beginning they had watched her with suspicion, ready to defend their pitches against a young and attractive new-comer. Now she was accepted as a mildly eccentric girl who minded her own business and never attempted to interfere with theirs.

Further along a group of women were discussing the threatened pregnancy of one of their number with much shaking of heads and clucking of tongues.

"Sixteen hours it took for the last one and my Mick pickled as a newt the entire time!"

"Wouldn't it be a splendid thing if you were to get a bed in the infirmary?"

"Don't talk like a fool, Peggy O'Brian! Isn't it only one step from the graveyard with those murdering doctors in that place!"

"Tansy? Tansy Malone?"

The sharp-nosed little figure in clerical garb was thrusting towards her with outstretched hand. For an instant she blinked in disbelief.

"Father MacNabb! What in the world are you doing in Liverpool?"

"I've been here a month already. There was talk of drafting in more priests to deal with the problems here, and I came on His Lordship the Bishop's instructions."

"But who's looking after the church at Perimara?"

Dismay had crept into her voice, for in all her remembered pictures of Perimara, Father MacNabb had always been there, stolid and immovable as his church. To see him on the dockside was like seeing the church itself uprooted and set down in an alien land.

"There's a curate there." The priest gave a mental impression of holding his nose. "A very smart young fellow from Dublin. Not that he has much to occupy his time. Surely there's hardly any congregation left at all!"

"Michael was hanged," she said in a small voice.

"Didn't I hear of it when I was after making enquiries in Dublin about your sister and yourself! You had no business to be leaving your home like that without a word to anybody."

He cast a sharp, suspicious look at her mended brown dress and tousled curls. Health glowed pink in her cheeks and her eyes were bright and clear.

"If we'd stayed we'd likely have starved, Father," she said.

"Aye, true enough; but how would you be living now? Do you have a decent, soul respecting job?"

"I work in an ale-house," she said bluntly. "Kate works at a milliner's, and we have lodgings over the shop."

It was better than he had hoped. Tansy had been a thorn in his flesh ever since she had been a child running free through the meadows of Perimara.

Bridie — God rest her! — had been sensible and serious and Kate had always had the air of a lady; but Tansy had been the one whom he was frequently forced to scold, the one who had bothered him with her questions and her impertinent retorts and her insistence on learning how to read and write.

He had hoped that her marriage to the steady, serious Michael O'Faolain would give her a sense of responsibility, but life had turned upside down, for it was Michael who lay dead in Dublin Gaol and Tansy, feckless as ever, who stood before and told him cheerfully that she worked in an ale-house.

"I hope you're being a good girl," he said with uneasy severity. "Going to Mass regularly, not neglecting the Sacraments?"

"We go every week," she said.

"And you're not getting into bad company? There are many temptations in the city for a young girl."

He spoke as if she were a small child instead of a widow

who would be eighteen in a matter of days.

"I earn an honest living," she said curtly, and added, to punish him, "And the Devereux, Father? Do you ever hear of them these days?"

At the mention of his patrons Father MacNabb's hollow cheeks flushed.

"Sir Raleigh and his good lady are in London, I believe," he said stiffly.

Their defection had been a sad disappointment to him. He still retained fond memories of Sir John Devereux who had plucked him as a barefoot boy from his cabin and made it possible for him to become a priest, but there was no denying that Mr. Raleigh was but a sorry echo of his father. There were tales of his constant gambling that Father MacNabb tried not to believe. Unfortunately it was impossible to overlook the fact that the Devereux had done nothing whatsoever to help their tenants.

"Have you had any news of your brother?" he asked, flicking the conversation into a less painful channel.

"Of Seamus?" Tansy shook her head. "We've had no word of him or Molly since they walked out with the rent money. The two of them never cared much for anybody except themselves."

"But Kate is well?"

"So pretty that she doesn't look real!" Tansy said with enthusiasm. "And she's much stronger than she used to be."

"I am happy to hear it." He looked at her with guarded approval. "I take it that neither of you is — er, contemplating marriage?"

Tansy wondered briefly what he would say if she told him about Jan Harrow and Donal the fiddler.

"Surely we're too busy earning an honest living," she said innocently.

He eyed her doubtfully. "I'm glad to hear it. If I had more time at my disposal surely I'd be visiting you both, but my hands are full with all the work there's to do here; reports to write, His Lordship to see — there's to be a redistribution of parishes."

"And food? Will they be distributing that too?"

"The care of souls is my province," Father MacNabb said quellingly.

"Oh, I see."

He had not, she thought, changed very much or learned very much. There was a kind of sick bewilderment in his small eyes as he glanced about him.

"Surely, when you get back to Perimara everything will be sorted out," she encouraged.

"One can only hope so." He gave a little sigh as if he held out very little hope for the village after the curate had finished with it. "I am bound for the harbour-master's office this morning. Some sort of check ought to be kept on the numbers arriving."

"Then I'll see you again perhaps, Father?"

"No doubt, no doubt."

He was bustling away, a sad little shadow of a man unable to cope with the changes thrust upon him. It had been, she thought, like falling over a small part of her own past. At least she could be sure that there would be little point in returning home. Perimara, with a curate in charge and the Devereux family gone, sounded so unlike the village where she had grown up that a little of her homesickness died. Perhaps after all it was better to be alive in the city than dying of hunger in blackened fields.

Jan Harrow came a few days later with gifts for both Kate and herself. The girls fingered their new shawls with pleasure, Kate's being in a soft blue, checked with pink; Tansy's shadow-striped in orange and brown.

"I know it's not done for gentlemen to give presents of garments to ladies," he said, "but the shawls being so pretty I figured you might accept them."

"And it's not as if they were," Kate blushed delicately, "intimate garments."

"They're grand, and we thank you kindly." Tansy pirouetted in hers, ends flying loose. "Will you be taking us to the theatre in them?"

"Tansy! It's polite to wait until you're asked."

Kate was half-shocked, half-laughing.

"I'd be glad to take you," he said promptly. "After all there's no telling when it'll be the last time."

"Mother of God! are you going to die too!" Tansy exclaimed.

"Not for another fifty years, I hope." A grin lighted his pleasant face. "But I've nearly worked my ticket. A few more trips and it's back to being a landlubber for me."

"Back to America? Then you really are going to work in your father's store!"

There was frank disappointment in Tansy's voice. Next to travelling in strange countries herself it was exciting to have a close friend who did these things.

"I guess I've had my fill of going back and forth across the Atlantic," he apologised. "Wanting to go to sea in the first place was a kind of rebellion, I guess. Well, I got it out of my system and I'm grateful to my father for not standing in my way. But the old man's getting on now; his heart's not what it was. And it'll please him to think there's somebody to carry on when he retires."

"Couldn't you put a manager in and still go travelling?" Tansy asked.

"Sure I could, but the urge to go travelling has kind of died in me. I guess I'm a shopkeeper at heart."

"I think it's splendid of you," Kate said warmly, "to sacrifice yourself to your family's interests in this way. It will make your father's last years very happy."

"We're hoping he'll last a good while yet." Jan turned to Tansy, his face mildly enquiring. "You said something about me going to die, too? I hope there's no bad news of any of your friends?"

"A dear friend of ours is gravely sick," Kate said.

Tansy gaped a little. To describe the ugly and massive Edward as 'a dear friend' sounded odd coming from Kate, who had scarcely exchanged a word with him during their lodging at the *Black Boy*, and who had given the ale house a wide berth since her departure.

"Edward manages the saloon where Tansy works," Kate was explaining. "It's been a great comfort to know that she's had somebody to look out for her interests there. But the poor man is very ill, I'm afraid. He has started to give away his property. He gave Tansy two hundred pounds towards her dowry which was very generous of him, don't you think?"

"I gave half of it to you," Tansy reminded her.

"She insisted that I take it," Kate said. "Tansy was always the most generous of sisters, but I could not help feeling that she ought to have kept the money. After all

127

Edward is more her friend than mine."

"But that's foolishness!" Jan spoke warmly. "She could not possibly keep so much money for herself!"

"It never entered my head!" Tansy said indignantly.

"It was very good of her anyway," Kate said. "I shall always be grateful. At least it means we're not entirely paupers."

"Why, nobody ever said we were," Tansy said in bewilderment.

"Though it's hard to live under somebody else's roof and have to work for one's living." Kate looked up with the shine of tears in her grey eyes.

"I reckon you two ladies are just about the bravest I know!" Jan said with enthusiasm.

Why, the poor man is a fool, Tansy thought. What kind of life does he think we had in Ireland? Doesn't it enter his head that we didn't work because there was no work?

"We do our best," Kate was saying. There was a little smile on her lips and her head was up, bravely defying a cruel world.

Tansy restrained a snort of derision and said airily, "Well, I'm off to see my dear friend. Opening time waits for no man!"

"Shall I escort you?" Jan asked eagerly.

"Holy Mother, no! Stay and talk to Kate." She gave them both a disapproving grin. "I'll be late tonight, so don't wait supper for me."

Rather to her surprise there were angry tears in her eyes as she ran down the narrow stairs. It was, she decided, a sign of her own pettiness that she should resent Kate's gentle evasions of the truth and Jan's acceptance of it. She herself never spoke of Ireland, but Kate's own memories of it were evidently coloured by time. She had forgotten how the roof of the Malone cabin had leaked in winter and how she had coughed when the wind blew the peat smoke the wrong way. She had wiped out of her mind Bridie's constant nagging and the boys' drinking and the everlasting struggle to find and pay the rent money.

"Miss Tansy, are you going out with your friend tonight?"

Conrad Schindler had emerged from the inner room and stood blinking at her. As always Tansy experienced a faint shock of surprise whenever she saw him. The old man came and went so quietly, so seldom intruding upon their conscious lives that it was difficult to realise that he lived in the same house.

"I'm going to work, Mr. Schindler,'. she said politely. "Was there anything you were wanting?"

Occasionally, in return for a nip of brandy, he lent her a book from his own collection downstairs. These were volumes in much better condition than the ones in her own room, and he was fussy about the handling of them. These exchanges, rare as they were, gave both of them a kind of guilty pleasure, for Kate thought book-reading a waste of time and was as hot against the drink as Bridie had been.

"I was wondering if you had to go out this evening," he said.

"I've my work to do," she said, puzzled.

Edward never questioned her infrequent absences or held her strictly to time, but the money he had given her and the resulting sense of obligation she felt made her hesitate when the temptation not to go in came over her.

129

"It might be wise," he said in his slow, careful way, "not to go among crowds for a little while. I'm told there is sickness in the dock area."

"There's always sickness," she said, amused and touched by his thinking of her. "They're overcrowded down there and the drinking water's none too fresh."

"This is a different kind of sickness," he said gravely. "This is what is known as cholera. You have heard the word?"

"Yes, of course, but I never knew anybody who had it." She looked at him in alarm. "How did it get here in the city?"

"The father of one of my pupils tells me today that a ship from Dumfries brought some immigrant families here a few days ago. The children were sick when they landed, but no check was made. Now two of them have died and there is talk that others from the ship are also affected. It is cholera, the authorities say. A disease that spreads more quickly and more terribly than you can imagine; so it would be wise to avoid crowds."

"I'm not likely to come to any harm," she assured him. "It's not as if I live down there, after all."

"But take care. I would not have — it would be a great grief to me if you were to fall sick, Miss Tansy," he said awkwardly.

"I'll take care," she said again, and let herself out into the street.

A dim blue twilight hazed the city and the emerging gaslights made little points of flame in the shadows. A couple strolled by, arms entwined, mouths open in laughter. Lower down the city stirred into life, spilling its citizens out into the courts and alleys.

Tansy drew her shawl over her head and cast a brief glance back towards the lighted window behind which Kate and Jan Harrow sat talking. She hoped Mr. Schindler wouldn't alarm her sister with talk of death and disease. As for herself — no sense in fretting until the worst happened.

NINE

Fear crept through the city, darkening the spring sunshine, making each day an ordeal to be faced with humour or despair according to one's nature. The sermon in church on the first Sunday in May was brief.

"God has laid His Hand upon the people of this place, smiting them as He once smote the mighty Egyptians. I urge each and every one of you to seek out the evil in your own hearts so that, if you are called, you may be ready to meet your Maker. In the Name of the Father —"

The priest's voice trailed into a mumble as he sketched a neat sign of the cross in the air and stepped briskly back to the altar to continue the Mass.

Ever since I can remember, Tansy thought, I've been sitting in churches listening to priests telling me how wicked we all are and how God is punishing us.

She felt depressed and low-spirited. Business at the ale-house was booming, which meant she was run off her feet most nights of the week and, when she slept, her dreams were troubling visions of a nightmare world where red biddy turned to blood and children wept unceasingly for parents who would never return.

"When there's trouble people drink deep to forget," Malachy said, rubbing his hands together with satisfaction.

He was as urbane and smiling as ever, seemingly unaffected by the misery that lay only a few yards from his door. Disease was useful for trade and he was the last person to scorn a profit.

"Is it true that three hundred people died last week?" Tansy asked.

"About two hundred and fifty, spread over the month. People always exaggerate."

Malachy yawned and settled himself more comfortably in the armchair by the kitchen fire.

"Something ought to be done," Annie said fretfully. "It's not decent having folk dying all over the place!"

"If you don't get the cholera you'll likely get the clap. Where's the difference?"

Maggie spoke dispiritedly, her lank yellow hair straggling over her face.

"Hark at you two! Haven't you had more clients these past weeks than you can handle?" Malachy exclaimed.

"It's not decent," Annie complained, "for folk to act that way with death just around the corner!"

"It's natural," Malachy allowed. "Get another cup of tea, Maggie, and put a spot of whisky in it. Alcohol is a great preventive of disease, my darlings!"

"Then you should be immune for life!" Tansy said pertly and dodged through the door before the cushion aimed by Malachy could find its target.

In the bar Edward was counting bottles with a gloomy expression on his heavy face.

"We need some extra deliveries," he said. "They're

drinking us dry, and there's a rumour that supplies are held up in the docks. The men won't unload the stuff until their rates of pay are upped. That means they'll draft in more Irish labour, and then there'll be trouble!"

"There's always trouble," Tansy said, and went to the window and stood on tiptoe to look out.

"Well, I'll not be here to see it." Edward straightened up with a little grunt of pain. "I've decided there's no sense in waiting around to catch another disease when I've already got one. I draw the line at dying twice over."

"But where are you going?" she asked in dismay.

"None of your business, girl," he said, and promptly relented. "To Wales, if you must know. My mother's people came from those parts, so I might have some relatives there — not that I'll trouble to look them up."

"It will seem strange without you here," she said.

"The place will survive. Malachy will get in a new manager, or do some work himself for a change. If you've any sense you'll get out, and marry one of your young men."

"I'm not afraid of the sickness," she said.

"Then you're a fool. I tell you, girl, there's nothing worse than waiting for it to creep up on you and strike you down. I've seen it before, seen a man tremble a little and complain of the cold and by nightfall he's a wreck of a being, lying in a pool of his own vomit with the water running out of him and the flesh dropping from his bones."

He spoke harshly, his ugly hands shaking as they moved bottles into place.

"You're afraid, aren't you?"

Tansy spoke wonderingly, for it had not occurred to her

that a man could face one kind of death with courage, yet shrink from another.

"There's no dignity in such a death," Edward said stiffly. "You'd do well to leave when I do. We neither of us owe Malachy O'Leary a thing."

"That wasn't the tune you sang when I pulled you out of the convict hulk," Malachy said from the doorway. "It was all gratitude then, wasn't it? You should have seen him in those days, Tansy. Half-starved and wolfish, with marks on his ankles where the leg-irons had bitten. Ripe for hanging or transportation or any other sweet wickedness, till I greased the palms of the local magistrates and you were set free in my custody."

"You've been repaid," Edward said. "I've run your stinking bar and looked out for the poor wretches that you and Florrie hound on to the beat. I don't owe you anything now. I'd have served my sentence by this time."

"And we won't talk about the nature of the crime, eh, Edward?" A gold tooth in Malachy's upper jaw glinted. "At least I've never had to worry about the girls, have I?"

The two stood eye to eye, glaring, their breath mingling in an angry rhythm. Something ugly and yet curiously intimate had sprung up between them. Tansy stood forgotten, her eyes flickering between the two men.

"I'm going, Malachy," Edward said. "I've no mind to lay a finger on you but I swear I'll kill you if you come after me. The girl is leaving, too. I'm not such a fool that I don't know what'd happen to her the minute my back was turned."

"The girl stays," Malachy said flatly. "I've fed her day in, day out, for nearly two years."

"And I've worked for every bite," Tansy said loudly. "Worked long and hard without pay. I don't owe you a thing either, Malachy O'Leary."

"Isn't that like a woman," he mourned, "to throw my kindness in my face!"

The threatened violence had passed but ugliness still hung in the air. A shaft of sunlight pierced the dark-panelled saloon and set the bottles twinkling against the big mirror. There had been a mirror in the tavern at Perimara once. The men had gathered there in the long, light evenings to drink poteen and grumble over the high rents. Their voices were stilled now, their laughter diminished, and her own face in the mirror was hard and strained as the child Tansy's had never been.

"I'm grateful for your help," she said placatingly. "I'm grateful, Malachy. I'm grateful to Edward, too, for being good to me. But it's time to move on."

Childishly, she wanted everything to end on a friendly note without bitterness. Edward gave her an exasperated look.

"No need to make a performance of it, girl," he said tersely. "Just take your things and go."

"And don't think you can claim any of your tips," Malachy put in. "You're leaving without notice so that means you forfeit your bonus, darling!"

"I don't want it." She caught the warning glint in Edward's eye and closed her lips firmly on the words, *I have a hundred pounds!*

"And don't come trailing back asking for another job." Malachy's voice was spitefully soft.

"I won't."

She hitched her shawl further over her head, and cast a swift look around the bar. Everything was neat and scrubbed and shining, but she had never imagined that Edward would walk out leaving anything in disarray. She wished she could think of something to say that would tie everything else up neatly, but the two men were staring at her again as if she were no more than an interruption on the surface of their lives.

"Say goodbye to Florrie and the girls for me," she said curtly, and pushed open the swinging door.

The sign above creaked in the wind as if it too bade her a grumpy farewell, and then she was in the street again. In a few minutes the first customers of the day would drift into the bar. She wondered if they would enquire her whereabouts and if Edward would stay for a few days longer until Malachy had put in another manager. But it was no longer any of her concern. She had come out of it well, she considered, with a dowry safely in Conrad Schindler's care, and a face that was just a little harder than the face she had possessed upon her arrival.

"You look like a sensible girl," a voice approved. "Can I trust you to run an errand for me? There's sixpence for you if you'll go."

An elderly woman, leaning on a stick, had picked her way through the rubble of a nearby alley, and now put a bony hand on Tansy's arm.

"A message? What message?"

"Run to the infirmary and tell Bessie O'Grady her youngest has been taken bad and she's to come home. You run and tell her to come. Your legs are better than mine, and I can't find anybody else who'll go."

"The infirmary?"

She had never been inside the gaunt building that stood cheek by jowl with the iron-doored workhouse, though she had passed it in her walks.

"You know where it is, don't you?" The woman peered at her, rheumy-eyed. "You'll go, won't you?"

"Yes, of course."

It was the last thing she wanted to do, but the woman's grip was painful, her voice urgent.

"Bessie O'Grady's youngest. Hurry!"

The grip was relaxed, and Tansy was hurrying as she had been bidden towards the upper streets of the city.

The first thing that met her as she went through the wide doors was a smell compounded of so many other smells that she could recognise nothing about it save its vileness. The hall with its speckled brown walls and peeling dado had an unutterably depressing aspect, and the passages leading from it stretched into darkness past narrow, closed doors with heavily carved handles.

Just inside the entrance two women with stained white aprons over their dresses and large mob caps on their heads were talking in low voices, that ceased as Tansy approached them.

"I have a message for someone," she said uncertainly. "Someone called Bessie."

"Would that be Bessie O'Grady?" one of the women enquired.

"Yes. Do you know her?"

"She's a cleaner here. If you want to see her she'll likely be in the sluice."

The woman pointed down the corridor and resumed her

muttered conversation.

The corridor was dim and evil-smelling, its floors worn by feet and scrubbing-brushes to a dingy grey. Halfway along a door opened abruptly and a man in a shabby frockcoat, holding a bunch of herbs close to his nose, came out with a silent, hurried step. Behind his shoulder Tansy caught a brief glimpse of a long room crowded with iron-railed beds and low pallets. Then the door closed again and he pushed past her with a muttered sentence that she couldn't catch.

"I beg your pardon, but I'm looking for the sluice," she raised her voice to call after him.

"First on the right. Put your mask up."

"Mask?"

"Regulations were made to be obeyed," the man said testily. "You people will never learn the elementary precautions! Wash your hands before you go back into the ward."

He was gone before she could explain or ask questions, his coat-tails flashing around the corner. Somewhere in the high echoing building a woman began to sob. The sobbing came quite clearly through the silence and was as abruptly hushed.

The place terrified her more than any place she had ever been in. In the hold of the ship they had all crouched together in mutual hunger and fear. But this place was impersonal with nothing to hold back the despair.

"Are you Bessie O'Grady?"

She pounced in relief upon a faded little woman who came, bucket-laden, around the corner.

"That's my name?"

The woman's voice was weary as her thin face and bowed shoulders.

"I've a message for you. Your youngest is taken bad, your neighbour says."

"Not Kevin?"

"Your youngest, she said. You're to hurry."

"Not Kevin? He's only six years old. I left him this morning and he'd only had a bit of a fever."

The woman stood before her, the buckets still clenched in her hands, her eyes blank with shock.

"You'd best go home," Tansy began.

But the woman said in a voice from which all colour had fled, "I have to carry the water to Ward Four. The doctor will be wanting it."

"I'll take it. You go home now."

Tansy seized the buckets and the woman moved past her like a sleep-walker. Only her lips continued to shape the words.

"Not Kevin? Kevin is only six."

"Bring that water here, girl, and try not to spill more than half of it!"

The new voice was sharp and self-confident, its owner a buxom being in lace-frilled cap and striped petticoat. Meekly Tansy followed her back along the passage and up a flight of iron stairs beyond which double doors gaped into a long room packed with the iron beds and low mattresses she had glimpsed before.

"Hurry up! What are you waiting for?" The woman had paused and was frowning impatiently.

"The smell — the awful smell!"

Tansy could barely get out the words for her stomach

was heaving, her teeth clenching in protest as bile rushed into her throat.

"You ought to cover your mouth and nose like the doctors tell us."

The woman was evidently more kindly disposed than she sounded for she came back to Tansy's side, pulling a small bottle from beneath her apron.

"Take a good swig," she invited. "It's the only way I can get through the day, believe me."

The gin stung her throat and tears poured down her cheeks.

"Give the buckets over here," she went on, "and go and give Mary a hand with that patient. He's too heavy for her to lift by herself."

It was a nightmare of blood and vomit and moaning delirium and skeleton hands held up in a last, desperate attempt to seize at life. They lay, two and sometimes three, to a mattress, their eyes glaring, their lips cracked for want of water, their noses sharp in sunken faces.

A hand clutched at her skirt and she whirled about, staring at a girl who whimpered through blackening lips.

"A priest. Holy Mother, will you not be after getting me a priest!"

There were priests there. She had seen two of them moving serenely between the packed rows, their faces calm, their eyes deep-shadowed with weariness. One of them stepped towards her and without surprise she recognised Father MacNabb. It seemed quite natural that he should still be in Liverpool, for he too had become a figure in the nightmare.

"I'll see to the poor child," he said in his precise

141

fashion. "Wait for me by the door, there's a good girl."

The way to the door was longer than she could have believed. Her legs moved slowly as if she were in a treacherous fog and the constant moaning beat in her ears like the sound of the sea. Somebody caught at her arm.

"Where's Bessie? She was due back here to lend me a hand."

"Kevin is sick," Tansy said.

"God in Heaven, a hospital full and she rushes off to one brat!"

The woman who had spoken spat vigorously into a pile of blood-soaked bandages, and turned again to her task of sponging the naked body of a child whose ribs strained pitiffuly through the thin layers of sweat-soaked flesh.

Somehow Tansy reached the door again, and leaned there against the peeling plaster of the wall. Her legs shook beneath her, and her head ached until the room spun round, tilting crazily first to one side and then to the other.

"Have you nothing better to do than stand there gaping?" another woman asked sharply.

"I'm waiting for somebody," Tansy said faintly.

"The only way anybody gets out of this hell-hole is feet first," the woman observed, "so you've a long wait ahead."

She had moved away before Tansy could think of a reply. Not that it mattered, for in this place people came and went with no more than a casual word or a passing glance. They were, she thought sadly, too weary for pity or curiosity.

"I have a message for you," said Father MacNabb,

bobbing up at her side again.

"For me? Who would send me a message?" She focused her eyes with difficulty on his narrow face.

"A friend of yours was brought in this morning. He was calling your name at any rate, and I don't know of anybody else with such a heathen title." He gave her a deeply disapproving look as if he held her entirely responsible for her name. "Be that as it may, the young man was calling for you. He kept on saying that you would come if you knew he was here."

"But who is he? Why wasn't I told?"

"Because, even if I'd known where to find you, I don't have the time to go running around the city delivering messages. There's an infirmary full of sick and dying people here, child."

"I'm sorry, Father," she said mechanically, "but the young man? Where is he?"

"I believe they put him in the side ward," Father MacNabb pointed vaguely towards a smaller door. "He would insist on bringing his fiddle with him."

She had gone before the sentence was fairly out of his mouth, before she had fully understood its import so that the meaning of his words didn't hit her until she stood in the narrow ante-room, retching as the stink rose up about her, hearing all around her the gurgling breath of the dying.

Donal was wasted skin and protruding bone with empty eye sockets and one hand clenched tightly, even in death, on the battered fiddle case. Nobody had drawn down his eyelids or smoothed a sheet above him. His body arched still as if in furious protest against the act of dying.

She dropped to her knees beside the filthy mattress, and spoke softly, urgently, as if he could still hear.

"I would have come if I'd known you were sick, Donal. I'd have come if Father MacNabb had given me the message, but he didn't know where I was. I would have come to you, Donal."

But she had not seen the fiddler for weeks, nor ever gone back to his room in Lace Street.

"There were two in the lodging dead with him when we got him out," Father MacNabb said at her shoulder. "I gave him the Last Rites, though he was past making Confession."

"He had nothing to confess," she said dully. "He never did a mite of harm in his life."

"He called out your name strongly enough," the priest said. "Was there nothing then between you?"

"Nothing that was sin," she told him.

Nothing but kindness and a need to be held safe, and a house on a hill that would never now be built.

"Will nobody see to the disposal of his body?" she asked, meeting the clouded, dead, reproachful gaze.

Her own fingers crept out towards the sunken face but would move no further to touch the dead flesh.

"We'll cover him decently," Father MacNabb said.

"And sell the fiddle to buy a proper coffin? I'd not have a friend lie in a pauper's grave."

"Holy Mother of God, child, does it matter where a man lies if his soul is at peace?" Father MacNabb asked irritably. "The fiddle is broken anyway, and even if it were not, 'twould hardly fetch enough to pay for a coffin."

"I suppose not."

She stood up again, remembering to cross herself as if she had prayed, but her heart was cold. Almost indifferently she watched the priest bend to close the eyes and wrench the stiffening hands together. Donal and the fiddle were broken now and there was no sense in weeping.

"Are you going home again, Father?" she asked, as they left the room.'

"Wouldn't I be there now if this sickness hadn't broken out and tied my hands!" he exclaimed. "That young curate will be letting the parish run to rack and ruin if I delay too long."

"But you don't have to stay?"

"Somebody must give comfort to the dying," he snapped. "I tell you there are not enough priests to go around, and the good Sisters are run off their feet! Would you believe it, but yesterday I had a Quaker woman helping me? A Quaker! I had to keep reminding myself that Our Blessed Lord kept worse company."

"So you'll stay."

But she had known that he would, just as she had known that Edward would leave, and Malachy hang on to his profits and Donal die with his music unheard.

"I cannot stay," she said. "I am — not big enough, Father."

"You have a duty to your sister," he said sternly. "Kate must be your first concern now."

He was right, of course. It would be wicked to carry the sickness to Kate. Already she could imagine the disease clinging to her hair and hands.

"And nursing is no task for a decent girl," he went on. "It's my personal belief that half the women here are creatures of misfortune, and no better than they should be. Now be off home and God bless you!"

He sketched a salute and hurried back into the ward, his head thrusting forward as if he were smelling out sin. Two men, covering a stretcher from which a naked, filthy foot protruded, went past her.

She went shakily down the stairs and into the long passages again. Once she stumbled over a couple huddled together against the wall. They were drinking from a shared bottle, but she could smell the decay on them.

Outside people were going about their business, though she fancied that a woman drew her skirts hastily aside as Tansy emerged from the infirmary. The air was warm and sweet, and further up the hill a few sprays of green forced their way through the cracks in the high walls of the lunatic asylum.

She would, she decided, go home and wash herself and put on the red dress. No need to upset Kate by telling her about Donal yet. But she would ask Conrad Schindler if he would join them for supper, and after supper they would persuade him to tell them stories in the firelight. It would be a strange sort of wake with only herself to know they were mourning anybody at all.

She'd have to tell Kate that she's given up her job. Kate would be pleased even though it meant stretching two extra meals a day out of the housekeeping. Too late Tansy remembered her own money, locked securely in the safe. A little of that would have bought Donal a grand coffin, but her duty was to the living, and she hastened her pace towards Dryden Street.

TEN

"It was a wise decision, Miss Tansy." Conrad Schindler put the tips of his fingers together consideringly. "You have no experience of nursing, my dear, and there are sights in a hospital to which no young girl should be exposed."

"They smelt like —"

She made a hopeless, fluttering gesture with her hands, and her eyes were full of remembered horror.

"You must not think of it." His voice held a tinge of sternness. "And you must not frighten Miss Kate with such tales."

"No, of course not."

Kate, she thought wearily, must always be protected.

"But it was sad for your friend; most sad." He fixed his spectacles a little more firmly on his nose and gave her a faintly inquisitive look. "He was, perhaps, more than a friend?"

"He would have liked to have been."

"But a strolling musician — that is no husband for a young lady who wishes to get on in the world."

"If I had loved him," she said miserably, "It wouldn't

have mattered at all."

"You and I must talk a little," he said, as if he had come to some private decision. "Shall we sit down and drink some tea?"

Kate had gone out on one of her rare shopping expeditions and the room at the back of the shop was comfortably untidy. Tansy went ahead of him through the concealing curtain, and busied herself with cups and saucers.

It was a relief to have something to do, for in the week she had spent at home, time had hung heavily on her hands. There was also in the old man's voice some tone of warning as if he contemplated reading her a lecture. It was, she thought, rather as if she were one of his pupils who had neglected to learn a lesson.

"Have you thought what you will do?" he began.

"Do? No, I haven't."

She had thought of nothing for a week, but the crowded fever wards and Donal's fingers stiffening on the fiddle.

"You will perhaps marry the young American?"

"He hasn't asked me yet," she said lightly.

On his last visit they had walked out together in Raneleagh Gardens, and he had taken her hand and talked about his father's house in Boston.

"Not that it's right in the middle of the city. My mother is a great one for her garden. She has grown anything you ever heard of in that orchard. My father says it keeps her out of mischief when he's down at the store. But the house itself is real nice — brownstone, with a bow window in the drawing room, and a sun-parlour at the back. She keeps the kitchen door open and the scent of her baking drifts through the passage."

"I'd love to see it!" she exclaimed.

"I'd like you to see it — I'd like both of you to see it," he responded. "I've told my family so much about you."

"Your sisters too?"

"They're wild to meet you. Did I tell you that Gerda's to be married?"

She shook her head.

"She's marrying a New Yorker, so she'll be leaving Boston. Sigrid will miss her. They went everywhere together. My folks say it would be real fine if I took a sweetheart home myself and we made a double celebration."

His voice ended on a shy, questioning note and his glance was warm.

"That would be lovely," she'd said, and lapsed into an idiotic giggle.

He'd spoken of the matter no more, but that evening she'd noticed him glancing between her and Kate as if he were evaluating them in his mind.

"He hasn't asked me yet," she repeated. "I think he wants to wed, but part of him wants to please his family, and he can't make up his mind if Kate or I would suit him better."

"He's right to think the matter over carefully." The reproving tone was back in his voice as he accepted the cup of tea. "It is a serious matter to choose a good wife."

"I suppose so." She sipped her own tea gloomily, her head bright in the dimness.

"But he will have to make his choice soon," the old man mused. "He will be returning to his home in a month or two, will he not?"

"The trouble is," she confided, "that the three of us are nearly always together! He fixes his mind on me and then he looks across the room and sees Kate. He gets talking to Kate, and I walk in."

"If one of you were wed or promised already, his path would be more simple," he mused.

"Well, they're hardly standing in line at the door," she said wryly. "I can't think of anybody who's waiting to run one of us up the aisle."

"There is myself," he said, so quietly that she was not certain she had heard him correctly and so sat with her mouth open, gaping at him.

"I am not a young man," he said unnecessarily. "In your eyes I am perhaps elderly, but at my age it is pleasant to have companionship. It was — lonely here before you and your sister came. There were too many memories of Rosa; and of Rebecca. It is not good, Miss Tansy, for a man to live with only memories."

"We're both grateful to you for giving us a home," she said, her voice edged with panic.

"You have made it a home again for me," he said. Everything is so clean and bright now."

"That was Kate. She's very good at housework!"

"It is cheerful again, too, and for that I think you are to be thanked."

"Father MacNabb was always on at me for being light-minded," she said.

"I have often known that you were tired, but always you have been cheerful and smiling," he went on as if he had not heard. "In your ways you are something like my Rebecca. She too loved to read and to wear pretty colours.

That is why I worried so when the fever came."

"Rebecca died of cholera, didn't she?" Until that moment she had forgotten the fact.

"It grows worse every day," he said sombrely. "More and more people dead."

"I know. There's a fever ship moored in the river. They're taking the worst cases there now."

If she could go on talking about the epidemic perhaps the extraordinary ideas that were rushing through his brain would vanish.

"It will grow worse still. Many are leaving the city."

"I know."

She had seen the carriages strung out along the road.

"This shop does not pay well," he told her. "Miss Kate has done her best, but the heart went out of the business when my Rosa died. And the lessons I give — they bring in very little. It is best for me to sell now and begin again, taking my stock with me. I have begun again before in a strange country."

"A strange country?"

"If you or Miss Kate would agree to become my wife, I will book a passage in the *Saranak*."

"To America? The *Saranak* sails to the United States."

"The land of opportunity. Many are going there to escape from the hunger and the fever. There are many ladies going —"

"Who will need bonnets." Her mind leapt ahead of him.

"Either you or Miss Kate will marry Mr. Harrow," he said. "Is it not better that you should not be separated by an ocean? And is it not better that one of you should enjoy the protection of a husband when she sets out to a strange

151

land?"

"It's impossible," she said flatly. "Kate would never agree."

"It is for you to point out the advantages to her," he said briskly. "The marriage would not be — it would be in name only, you understand. At my age one does not contemplate —"

"So one of us is to marry you and leave the other a clear field with Jan Harrow? It sounds like a business arrangement!" she said indignantly.

"So it is, Miss Tansy. A business arrangement that would be profitable to both."

"But cannot one of us simply travel with you as your assistant?" she argued.

"And leave Mr. Harrow to drown still in his own indecision?"

"If he can't make up his mind, then he doesn't deserve either of us," she said.

"But it would be a good match for one of you," he said slyly.

Tansy was silent, biting her lip. She had heard of such marriages of convenience, of course, but in her own world folk married for love.

But you didn't, a thought mocked her. You married Michael O'Faolain because he was kind and pleasant, and you were used to him.

"You are not, I think, deeply attached to any man?" Schindler ventured.

Nor ever have been, Tansy thought with ruthless self-honesty.

There had been her brief, childish liking for Raleigh

Devereux, of course, but that had been a fleeting thing. Donal she had pitied, and even Jan Harrow — she liked the stolid young officer immensely, but she could contemplate his possible marriage to Kate with scarcely a pang of jealousy.

"I don't think I ever will be in love with anybody," she said slowly. "After all I'm past eighteen, so it's not likely I'd be fancying anybody now, is it? And even if I did, chances are that he'd not fancy me."

"Eighteen? My dear, I am sixty-three," Conrad Schindler said. "But King David took a young wife and lived in harmony with her."

"And you don't mind if it's Kate or me?"

"I have not the right to make the choice," he said simply.

"I'll talk it over with Kate."

She stood up, not certain if she were more embarrassed or amused. She had heard of old gentlemen getting strange notions before, but this —!

It was evening before she could tackle Kate and she found her sister in a pensive mood.

"They were saying at the butcher's that more than eight hundred people have died in the past week," she said. "Almost every house has straw outside the door and black crepe on the knocker."

"They're digging pits on the outskirts of the city," Tansy nodded.

"To tumble in the dead." Kate licked her lips nervously. "Those who can afford it have left. I was thinking it was time we talked of leaving too."

"We have a hundred pounds each," Tansy reminded her

"That wouldn't last for ever with prices so high and jobs so hard to find," Kate said. "We could hire ourselves out as servants somewhere perhaps, but in a city there's always disease."

"We could emigrate," Tansy said.

"All by ourselves? Don't be so silly, it wouldn't be proper!" Kate reproved.

"I was talking to Mr. Schindler this afternoon —"

"And that's another thing. Business has fallen off terribly. Nobody is interested in buying hats these days."

"Kate, *listen!* Mr. Schindler is thinking of selling the shop and going to the United States of America!"

"He's — what?" Kate broke off to stare at her.

"He told me he wants to sell the business and take his stock to America, to start again there," Tansy said patiently.

"You must have heard it wrong," said Kate.

"Surely I did not! And there's something more. He wants to marry one of us and take her with him."

"Tansy Malone O'Faolain, have you been at the poteen?" Kate asked suspiciously.

"It's true. He told me."

"That old man? What a disgusting idea!" Kate wrinkled up her straight nose.

"It's to be a marriage in name only," Tansy said hastily. "It will protect one of us and give him some companionship."

"And what's to become of the one he doesn't marry?" Kate asked.

"Why, she'll marry Jan Harrow," Tansy said.

"So Mr. Harrow is to have Conrad Schindler's leavings?

154

You seem to have arranged everything very nicely between the pair of you!"

There was a decided snap in Kate's gentle voice.

"It wasn't like that at all," Tansy said. "It's for us to make the choice, Kate. You know yourself that Jan Harrow means to take a wife.

"He told me about it. His family wants him to settle down, especially now that —"

"His sister is marrying a New Yorker and leaving home."

Tansy's amber eyes met her sister's grey ones and they both laughed suddenly.

"So Jan Harrow is fond of us both." Kate spread her hands slightly. "Well, he cannot wed us both."

"He will wed neither of us if we don't give him a little push," Tansy said firmly.

"Which means that one of us must stand aside. But to marry Mr. Schindler — that isn't necessary."

"He did take us in."

"And got an unpaid housekeeper and an unpaid shop assistant," Kate shot back.

"He won't take one of us to the States unless one of us marries him. He says it wouldn't be proper."

"Or profitable. A wife is cheaper to keep than an assistant. He'd get the dowry too."

"I'd forgotten that. But I don't believe it was in his mind either. He's just a lonely old man, Kate, and he's afraid of the cholera. His little girl died of it."

"I know." Kate's eyes softened.

"It's a long way to America. I'd not like to think of one of us on one side of the ocean and the other thousands of miles away," Tansy coaxed.

155

"But I'd be with Jan Harrow," Kate said.

"Oh? Who's to say he likes you better than me?" Tansy asked sharply.

"You have Donal."

"Donal's dead of the fever. He died a week ago."

"Dead? Oh, the poor man! And him so sweetly playing here!" Kate's lip trembled. "But you never said one word."

"He's dead. There wasn't anything to tell."

"Well, you're a queer one! Sometimes I think you haven't got any feelings at all," Kate said.

"I don't want to talk about him," Tansy said brusquely.

"The poor man!" Kate shook her head again sadly. "But there are other men, Tansy. You're so gay and pretty that lots of men will want to marry you one day."

"You're prettier than I am," Tansy contradicted.

"But I can never think of anything to say to young gentlemen. Now Mr. Harrow is so pleasant and frank that it's easy to talk to him."

"So you want me to stand aside?"

Tansy frowned, bringing her sister's delicate features so sharply into focus that they seemed for a moment to be carved out of stone.

"I'm the elder, and you've had one husband already," Kate pointed out.

"I met Jan Harrow first," Tansy said quickly.

"You can manage the reading and the writing," Kate said. "You could always earn a living. It isn't as if you loved Jan."

"It isn't as if you loved him either."

"But I could make him a good wife!" Kate said tearfully. "I've always wanted to live in a grand house, Tansy, and

156

wear pretty gowns. It's been so hard for me, having to leave my home and work in other folks' houses."

"I've worked hard too, alanna."

"I know you have," Kate leaned across to take Tansy's hand. "I'm grateful to you, more grateful than I can say. But you're fond of Mr. Schindler, and you'd enjoy helping him run a business is a new country. You know you would!"

"I'm fond of Jan too," Tansy said stubbornly.

She felt a little sick inside for this was the first time in her life that she had put herself before Kate. But Kate must be fair. She would have to understand —

"So we're equal, it seems," Kate said.

Her eyes were cool, her voice pleasant, but the sickness inside Tansy wouldn't go away.

"Do we toss pennies for it?" Kate asked in the same sweet tone.

"We'll play cards! There's a pack in the drawer."

Tansy jumped up, eager suddenly for action, for something to break the tension in the room. It was almost as if they had become enemies over two men neither of them loved.

"How shall we play?" she asked uncertainly.

"I don't think we ought to play at all," Kate said. "It's surely wicked to gamble anyway, and to gamble for a husband — does the idea not fill you with shame, Tansy?"

"No, it doesn't. It's shameful to go marrying for business reasons anyway, so we might as well go the whole road," Tansy said firmly.

"I don't know, I'm sure." Kate eyed the shiny pack doubtfully.

157

"We play cards when Jan Harrow comes," Tansy said.

"That's different. We don't play for money."

"We're not playing for money now," Tansy said reasonably. "We're playing for husbands."

"We'd never be able to tell them. They would think it dreadful of us," Kate warned.

"Donal would have laughed," Tansy said.

She could picture the crooked smile on his face, hear the gentle mockery with which he would have greeted such a gambling game. But the fiddler was dead and his music with him, and she had never wanted to be a part of his dream.

"I'm sure it's against the Faith," Kate worried. "I still feel that as I'm older than you —"

"Did any harm ever come from taking a chance?" Tansy demanded and rushed on without waiting for an answer. "We took a chance when we came over in the boat, and it turned out well. Oh, Kate, we have to get out of the city and whichever way we do it it'll come to the same thing in the end. We'll go to a new land, with work and friends and no more famine, no more fever. It will be the same for us both!"

"Except that one of us will be tied to an old man."

"It might be me. It might be me, Kate. We've an equal chance."

Kate hesitated a moment longer, her eyes restless, her normally pale skin flushed patchily red. Then she gave a little nod.

"Then let's have it over with. Shuffle the pack."

"Highest card wins," Tansy said. Her fingers trembled as the smooth pasteboard slid between them.

"Wins Jan Harrow?"

"Wins Jan Harrow."

She put the neat, rectangular pile down on the small table and looked across towards her sister.

Kate had paled again, her lower lip caught between her teeth, her fingernails tapping nervously on the edge of the table.

"Highest card wins!" Tansy said again.

There was a tight knot of fear and excitement in her stomach and little beads of sweat broke out along her hairline.

Kate leaned forwards and slid a card from the pile, turning it slowly face upwards.

"Eight of Hearts," she said flatly.

Tansy's own small hand advanced, pulled and twisted.

"Ten of Diamonds," she said on a little gasp of relief.

She didn't love Jan Harrow, but he was young and pleasant and she would make him a good wife.

"I'll shuffle this time," Kate said.

"Shuffle again?" Tansy looked up in surprise.

"It has to be the best of three," Kate said calmly. "You don't expect to be choosing a husband on the turn of one card, now do you?"

"I suppose not."

The tightness was back in her stomach and something behind her eyes stung unpleasantly.

"Your turn to choose first," Kate said, indicating the pile.

"It's a Knave of Clubs!"

Her voice was a joyous squeak.

"My turn now."

Kate flipped over the card and held her breath out in a long sigh.

"King of Hearts beats it," she said sweetly. "Your turn to shuffle, alanna."

The backs of the cards were patterned with pink flowers. They danced crazily in the candlelight.

"I'll let you choose first if you like. You were lucky in the first draw," Kate offered.

"What difference does it make?" Tansy asked crossly as she reached out.

The stinging behind her eyes had subsided into a dull aching misery.

"I'll take mine and then we can look at them together."

Kate's voice was as gay as if she had thought up the entire scheme by herself.

"King of Spades," Tansy said.

"And mine is the Ace of Diamonds. Ace counts high in this game."

"We never decided that," Tansy began.

"There was nothing to decide. Ace always counts high," Kate said gently. "Or do you want to draw another card? We can carry on all night if it pleases you."

"It doesn't matter."

Miserably, Tansy stared down at the card in her hand. The dark faces of the King stared back at her unblinkingly.

"Don't look like that," Kate begged. "Mr. Schindler is a kind old gentleman — didn't you say so yourself? And he has no relatives. Why, he might die and leave you a mint of money! And you won't have to get used to parents-in-law either! Jan's mother might not like me at all. And it isn't as if you have to — to sleep with the old man."

"And it isn't as if I were in love with anybody else," Tansy said, forcing a smile to her stiff lips.

"But you're very fond of Mr. Schindler," Kate urged. "He'll surely let you do as you please, and you must coax him out of some of his profits."

"If ladies in America buy bonnets," Tansy gulped.

"Surely they will! You're not going to sulk because you lost? That isn't like you at all, alanna."

"No, I'm not sulking." Resolutely she forced back the tears of disappointment that glittered on her lashes, and fixed a smile to her mouth. "But you can hardly expect me to be jumping for joy now."

"We'll be sailing to a new country," Kate said, "Didn't you always want to be travelling to foreign lands?"

"That's true."

But the room was gloomy still and her heart lay like a stone.

"Will you tell Mr. Schindler in the morning what we've decided and then when Jan comes I can tell him that you're promised?"

"Which will lead to your being promised yourself if everything goes well? That's another gamble," Tansy said dryly.

"Not a very big one. Jan Harrow only needs a little push to send him in the right direction," Kate said comfortably.

"Then it's settled."

The words had a hollow, final ring as if she had just slammed down her own coffin lid. But that was a foolish thought. At eighteen, she was still alive with years and years ahead of her. Years, her mind whispered, of being tied to an old man, of existing in a world where all that mattered was to sell bonnets and count the profits.

"Mr. Schindler won't want a big wedding, I daresay," Kate was saying thoughtfully. "But you'll have to have a new dress, and then I suppose Jan Harrow and I will be waiting until we reach Boston. An autumn marriage would be pretty, don't you think?"

ELEVEN

"It will be necessary to get all the details from the Government Emigration Office," Conrad Schindler said, "and book a passage on the *Saranak* as quickly as possible. There is a great rush for tickets, I believe."

"Mr. Harrow will be paying my fare," Kate said.

She sounded as snugly content as a kitten licking its paws in front of the fire. Only Tansy was aware of the long week of frustration she had endured, when Jan had called every day and not proposed marriage, even though the sisters had taken care to tell him of Tansy's betrothal.

"To marry Mr. Schindler?" he had echoed, unable to conceal the surprise on his face.

"Mr. Schindler has been so kind to us both," Kate had explained. "And Tansy always has preferred mature gentlemen. Her first husband was ten years older than she was, you know."

"No, I didn't." Jan gave Tansy an unhappy, embarrassed look. "I hope you will be very happy," he mumbled at last.

"Oh, he will spoil her and let her do exactly as she pleases," Kate said.

"And really to be off to the States!" he marvelled. "Well,

that will suit you just fine, Miss Tansy, but what gave the old gentleman such a notion?"

"The cholera epidemic," Tansy said. "Surely you saw the fever ship in the harbour?"

For all his pleasant ways Jan Harrow was a bit of a fool, she thought.

"I told them both that they had to go," Kate said. "Tansy must put her duty to her new husband before family loyalty. She has considered me for long enough."

The hint had been broad enough, Lord knows, but it had taken another five days before Kate had arrived back from a walk with Jan, her cheeks glowing, her eyes starry.

"Mr. Harrow has asked me to be his wife," she said primly, and collapsed into suddenly half-hysterical laughter.

"Tell me about it."

Tansy bounced up from the bed where she had sprawled with a book and put a wealth of pleasure and excitement into her voice. There was, after all, no point in spoiling Kate's delight with her own disappointment.

"He said he'd be surely honoured if I would agree to a formal betrothal at once. He's buying me a betrothal ring tomorrow morning. The *Saranak* sails on Thursday so there isn't much time."

"It's his last trip, isn't it?"

"He's going home to take over his father's store," Kate said. "He's already written to his family and told them he's going to wed me, so he must have been sure of my answer, mustn't he? And he wants me to travel over with you and Mr. Schindler. Have you decided where you're going to set up business?"

"In Philadelphia, I suppose. We haven't talked much about it."

They had not, she realised, talked about anything very much. Conrad Schindler, when she had told him of her readiness to be married to him, had patted her shoulder and remarked approvingly that she was a sensible young lady. A little later he had come to her and shyly put in her hand a pretty silver locket.

"In the old days Rosa wore it with a twist of Rebecca's hair inside. I have taken out the hair and the locket is yours now," he said.

It hung about her neck, small and heartshaped, its cavity empty.

Kate had returned the next morning with a diamond glinting on her hand. By her side Jan looked proud and ill at ease. It crossed Tansy's mind that he was a little alarmed at his own decision.

"We'll buy the wedding ring in Boston," Kate said. "Jan's mother has a beautiful lace veil that her grandmother wore so the family will want me to use that, I suppose. But I shall have a white satin dress."

Tansy had a new dress of brown silk with amber ribbons at neck and sleeves, and a bonnet of cream straw trimmed with the same ribbon. Conrad Schindler had taken the ring from his wife's dead finger and wore it on his own little one. During the ceremony he would slip it on to Tansy's finger below the tarnished circle Michael had put there.

"I'll feel happier knowing that Kate is travelling with you," Jan said.

"We'll take good care of her," Tansy promised, and the

coupling of herself with the old man sounded strange in her ears.

"At this season the voyage should be very smooth," Jan assured her. "They say that in a few years it'll all be steamships, but I doubt it myself. There has to be a limit to what men can do."

"But not to the ideas they have," Tansy said thoughtfully, and surprised a gleam of admiration in her future brother-in-law's eyes.

"It will be advisable to book a cabin for the young ladies," Conrad Schindler mused. "Miss Kate will not wish to share with strangers."

"But surely you and —"

Jan shut his mouth firmly and crimsoned as he glanced from Tansy to the old man and back again.

"As we are to be separated after we land, Tansy and I want to spend as much time together as we can," Kate said.

"Sure, sure!" Jan's voice was hearty, his eyes still puzzled.

Shortly afterwards, he had taken his leave, Kate going with him only to the front step, for she was terrified of the fever-laden air of the dockside.

Now, with the mortality figures rising higher as one warm day succeeded another, the three of them sat in the upstairs room discussing the details of their voyage. The shop had been sold for a much lower figure than Conrad Schindler had hoped, but the house was in need of repair and he had packed away his stock.

"We will begin in a small way when we reach America," he told the girls. "I intend to take lodgings for a month or two, and then to rent suitable premises. And it may also be possible for me to give lessons in German to one or two pupils."

It would be, Tansy thought, a neat and peaceful life. They would rent a modest place and she would help to make and sell the bonnets, and in the long evenings she would read and learn to cook, and Mr. Schindler would instruct any pupils he had managed to acquire. Thinking this, there rose up in her something that was neither neat nor peaceful, but wild and strong and discontented.

She had gone down one afternoon to the *Black Boy*, but the door was closed, the shutters pulled down, the sign hanging limply in the warm air. Edward had gone, and from the look of things Malachy and Florrie had fled too. She wondered if all three were dead and what had happened to Annie and Maggie and the half-witted Susan; and if Father MacNabb had returned to Ireland. But there was nobody she could ask and after a while she had trailed back up the hill, passing the black shrouded knockers of the little houses that cowered under the high walls of St. George's Hall.

Her few possessions were packed in a corded trunk that had once belonged to Rosa. Rosa's locket hung about her neck. On the next morning Rosa's widower would place Rosa's ring on her finger. Once or twice in an absent-minded moment Conrad Schindler had called her Rebecca.

I am, she thought, a replacement for his wife and for his daughter. I am no longer myself at all.

The tickets were bought, the passports delivered, the emigration forms filled in. The shop had been officially closed which merely meant that its few customers no longer came. Tansy had met the new owners, a rotund, placid couple who intended to start a little bakery and were apparently in no fear of catching any disease that might be hanging over the city. They had purchased the furniture too, so that only the books and the millinery stock had been crated.

"If Jan had not resigned his commission so soon he could have made the journey with us," Kate said.

"He's travelling from Boston to meet you in Philadelphia, isn't he?"

"Yes. He wanted to make sure everything would be perfect for me when I arrived. He's a wonderful man!"

Kate twisted the hoop of diamonds on her finger and let the corners of her mouth quirk upwards.

"He's that indeed," Tansy agreed.

"I am truly fond of him, you know," Kate said quickly as if she had been accused of something. "And it isn't as if you were in love with him yourself."

"That's true," Tansy said lightly.

"And you do wish me happiness, don't you? Say that you wish me happiness."

"All that you can get, alanna," Tansy said and a rush of warmth enveloped her being.

For all her beauty, Kate had never known the affection of a man nor the embrace of a lover. In Ireland the young men had admired her and kept their distance. In Liverpool she had spent most of her time in the dark, little shop. And she was twenty now, as pale and pretty as a delicate flower unvisited by a bee.

"I want you to be happy!" Tansy exclaimed again, lifting her hands as if she sought to brush away some shadow that lay between them.

"I only hope that Jan doesn't expect me to trail down and help in the store," Kate pouted. "Faith, but there's nothing worse than standing behind a counter all day! You had a livelier time of it than me."

"But you always said that you wouldn't work in a bar for anything," Tansy protested.

"Did I? Well, this place is dull enough in all conscience," Kate shrugged her shoulders, enquiring, "Have you everything ready for the morning? Does Father know the time of the service?"

"At midday. We sail on the evening tide."

"Lord be praised that Mr. Schindler agreed to baptism and instruction else you'd never have been married at all," Kate said fervently.

In less troubled times he would have had a harder task convincing the Church of his sincerity, but with funerals and deathbed rites eating up the day, the harassed little parish priest had rushed the old man from Judaism to Christianity without making more than the most perfunctory enquiries as to the state of his soul.

"It was very good of him," Tansy said mechanically.

The conversion, she knew, meant little to the man who had ceased to believe in anything at all, but if she told Kate that, her sister would be shocked. Kate still believed unquestioningly that the Creator was all good and all wise. Tansy, remembering the smell of the infirmary and Donal's dead eyes, knew only that He was all powerful.

"I'll bring you a cup of tea in bed in the morning," Kate promised, "and do your hair for you in the new style, puffed over the ears and twisted low at the back of your neck. It's such a lovely colour that it will suit you like that. It'll make you look more grown-up."

Nearer to the bridegroom's age, I suppose, Tansy thought dryly, but she didn't speak the words aloud for fear of being accused of sulkiness again.

To her own surprise, when the candles were extinguished, she found herself drifting easily into sleep. She had expected to toss and turn for hours, going over and over the events that had led up to this incredible marriage, but her bed was comfortable, her eyelids heavy, and there was no point in regretting what was to come.

The sun shone the next day and a heat haze blurred the city. Kate brought her tea and ham between thin slices of bread and butter, and sat on the edge of the bed while Tansy ate and drank. She was livelier than usual, chattering about a variety of subjects, a flush on her cheeks, her grey eyes bright. It was, the younger girl thought, almost as if Kate would be relieved to see the wedding safely over.

The hours of the morning dragged past very slowly, so slowly that Tansy began to hope that the time would never arrive. She kept on hoping while Kate helped her into the brown dress and coiled her long hair into the style that would make her look like a fashionable lady. And then Conrad Schindler, looking uncomfortably spruce in a new suit and fresh white linen, tapped on the door to tell them the hired brougham was arrived, and all hope was at an end.

She took her place next to Kate and smiled nervously at the old gentleman who within the hour would be her husband. He was, after all, a kind person and in giving his name and protection to a penniless girl he was doing a generous thing. Not quite penniless, her mind corrected, for she had had Edward's hundred pounds. Mr. Schindler had retained her share, but she supposed that if she ever needed it she could ask for it back.

"We're here," Kate said, and she began to hustle them into the church as if she feared something might occur to prevent the wedding.

Nothing did! And that was the worst of all, that nobody should come forward to protest that a girl of eighteen ought not to be joined to a man of sixty-three. The Service went forward without interruption from the first 'Dearly beloved' to the last 'Amen'.

A few people had wandered into the dim interior of the church, but they seemed more intent on their own prayers than on the gabbled words below the altar. The only person to congratulate the couple when they paced into the vestry was the local registrar, there to record the event for the civil authorites.

Signing her name in neat, round characters in the heavy register, Tansy wondered suddenly what Kate would do when it was her own wedding day. Did Jan Harrow realise that his lovely bride could neither read nor write? But then Kate was so beautiful that it probably didn't matter to him.

"May I wish you both every happiness, Mr. and Mrs. Schindler, and a safe and pleasant voyage?"

The registrar was shaking hands and Kate's cool cheek was pressed briefly to Tansy's flushed one. When they emerged into the sunshine a group of ragged urchins sent up a cheer. Further down the street a funeral cortège waited patiently, the black-plumed horses nodding their heads sleepily, the mutes top-hatted and sweating. She looked away sharply, unwilling to admit omens.

171

The shop was bare and clean. With a little pang of guilt Tansy realised that Kate had done most of the cleaning and packing, and done it without complaint while she herself had wandered aimlessly through the small rooms, picking up one thing and putting it down again in the same place.

There was a cold buffet laid on the table upstairs and Conrad Schindler produced a bottle of white wine. The three of them sat in an awkward silence, intensified by the tramping of feet below as the carters loaded the boxes and crates on to the wagon.

"I must take the keys next door so that the new owners may collect them," Conrad Schindler said.

He seemed to be glad of an excuse to leave the girls alone for a few minutes, but when he had gone to deposit the keys and to give final instructions to the carters, there was still nothing to be said.

Kate rinsed the dishes and stacked them neatly. Tansy sat pleating the brown silk of her wide skirt, her face concealed under the brim of her cream bonnet.

"It is time to be going, young ladies."

Conrad Schindler had returned, his expression anxious as if he feared they might have left something important behind. If memories of his dead Rosa and of Rebecca who had not lived to grow up filled his mind, he was too kindly to reveal it.

"We are quite ready," Kate spoke for them both, drying her hands on a little towel and hanging it neatly on the edge of the stone sink.

"We will be in good time, I understand," Conrad Schindler consulted his watch. "I believe our luggage will be dealt with very promptly and we will have leisure to examine our sleeping quarters."

He was unable to resist a last look around the room. Its cupboards were empty now, the books and linen crated, those dresses which had not been altered to fit Kate or Tansy donated to charity. After a moment he clapped his hands together softly as if he were ending a lesson and ushered the girls out to the waiting cab.

It was strange to rattle through the streets where she had walked and knew it was unlikely that she would ever see them again. The streets were almost deserted, for since the mortality rate had risen to a thousand the previous month, few people ventured out unless it was absolutely necessary. The docks, however, presented the usual bustle and confusion as long lines of emigrants were jostled and questioned by wan-faced children and harassed customs officials.

"We have reserved places and need not wait," Conrad Schindler told his companions as they alighted. "I must make certain our baggage has been checked and cleared. If you would stand near the gangplank I will be as quick as possible."

"It is, after all, an adventure to travel," Kate murmured. "But then, Jan will be meeting me, of course."

She gave Tansy an enquiring glance as if waiting for an answer, but finding none turned aside and began to pace up and down, her skirts held clear of the slippery quay in her gloved hands.

Jan Harrow would be meeting her, to whisk her away to a loving family who lived in a brownstone house and kept a store in the city.

And I, thought Tansy, could have kept my share of Edward's gift and started afresh somewhere. It's not likely I'd get the cholera at all. I didn't get it after I'd been to the infirmary, so it's hardly likely I'd fall sick now.

But she had been trapped by compassion for an old man's loneliness and by the feeling bred in her since childhood that Kate must be protected.

I am Tansy Schindler now, she thought bleakly, and was swept with anger against the world and against her own stupidity. Her brown eyes raked the gangplank with contempt, for of what value was adventure with no glittering prize at the end of it?

And then she was motionless, the anger burning into wonder, her lips parted on a soundless whisper, her hands still on the amber ruching of her gown. What was it that Edward had told her? Something about a wildness and a wishing and a knowing of love in a word or a glance.

The man standing on the gangplank was browner than any man she had ever seen; his skin glowing copper under the sun.

He was conventionally dressed in dark broadcloth with ruffles of white at neck and wrists, but there was nothing conventional in the face with its high cheekbones and jutting nose and wide mouth. It was a face in which savagery and tenderness were most oddly mingled, and to its conflicting qualities was added an expression of bitter, brooding humour.

No man, she thought in confusion, should stand so tall or so proud unless he owned the whole world. And no man should look at a lady as he is looking at me.

But she could not look away from the dark eyes that

174

held her own in a gaze that was both challenge and recognition. Yet she knew beyond all doubt that she had never met him in her life before.

A wishing and a wildness, she thought, and raised her head as if to repel an enemy even as her hands curved outwards as if to welcome a friend.

He was not smiling as his eyes held hers, but she knew already how he would look in laughter.

"Shall we go aboard, young ladies?" Conrad Schindler enquired, hurrying back towards them. "Our cabin baggage will be delivered to us very shortly."

"Tansy, do hurry! You look half-asleep," Kate said.

But she was more awake than she had ever been, with every nerve stretched to its limit, every desire throbbing through her slim frame as if she had been jerked out of an enchantment.

The man raised thin black brows and then gave a barely perceptible nod as if he set seal to a bargain between them.

"Hold the rope, my dear," Conrad Schindler was saying. "It can be quite treacherous as this angle."

Whatever of love and hate lies between us in the future I shall always remember this moment of knowing. Whatever parts us in days to come shall only serve to strengthen what begins between us now. Whatever your race or your dreams, I make them mine.

Silently she made her pledge and then, ahead of her ageing husband and her pretty sister, Tansy began to board the *Saranak*.

KATE ALANNA

MAUREEN PETERS

The hold of the ship is crammed with Irish people, escaping to Liverpool from the famine that has devastated their land. Among them are the Malone sisters, the gentle, ladylike Kate, and Tansy who has dreams in her eyes and a sharpness in her tongue.

But the city to which they come teems with new dangers, stinks of corruption and violence, and is menaced by cholera. In the twisting alleys and crowded docks, Tansy fights for survival and a better life for her sister and herself. And in this mid-Victorian world she meets many strange characters, who help or hinder her struggles. There is Malachy who procures girls, Donal the fiddler, Jan the American officer, and Conrad Schindler, the old Jewish milliner who plans to change her life.

It is only when Tansy has made her choice that events take a sudden and surprising turn, and the future of the Malones blossoms into the promise of a new adventure.

£2·70 net